Fate of the Gods

By

Jaden Sinclair

Published by
Melange Books, LLC
White Bear Lake, MN 55110
www.melange-books.com

Fate of the Gods, Copyright © 2012 by Jaden Sinclair

ISBN: 978-1-61235-447-7 Print

Cover Art by Caroline Andrus

Fate of the Gods
Jaden Sinclair

War affects us all. Some hold the memories of the past close to their hearts. The past has made Amelia the woman she is now. Second born daughter, she doesn't see herself as anything special, and on her sixteenth birthday she discovers just how special she isn't. However, one person reminds her she is just as special as anyone else.

Drakon Anthony didn't expect to get the wind knocked out of him by the young princess of Egypt or that a few years later she would bring him to his knees. One look at the beauty she has become and the battle within him to take her begins. He wants her, and she wants him, but politics within the kingdom might make wanting and having somewhat difficult, but will it make it impossible?

Contact the Author

www.jadensinclair.com

**Other stories by Jaden Sinclair
at www.melange-books.com**

The Proposal
Kiss Under the Mistletoe *in Holiday Treats*
The Christmas Dream in Wicked Christmas Wishes
S.H.I.L.O.
S.E.T.H.
Interplanetary Passion
Outerplanetary Sensations

SHIFTER SERIES
Stefan's Mark
Claiming Skylar
Dedrick's Taming
The Prowling
Cole's Awakening
The New Breed
Seducing Sasha
Draeger's Legacy

Lucifer's Lust, with Mae Powers
Love at First Sight

Tales of the Forbidden, Book 1, Forbidden Temptation
Tales of the Forbidden, Book 2, Forbidden Rapture
Tales of the Forbidden, Book 3, Forbidden Innocence

Pirate's Hellion
Raided Pleasures"

Prologue

9092 Egypt

Fire blazed through the town, women screamed, children cried and men ran everywhere. Some of the men were soldiers from the great house of Egypt and others were from the raid that was taking place now.

The smell of flesh burning and blood being spilled hung heavily in the air and in the middle of it all sat one little girl, crying over the fallen bodies of her parents. The King and Queen of Egypt lay in their own blood, lifeless eyes looking up at a dirty, teary-faced girl.

She watched helplessly as more of her parents' people fell to their deaths. The sight of black leather boots walking at a slow pace towards her made the little girl look up. A boy in his teens looked down at her with a sinister smile. In his hand he held a bloody sword—the blood dripping down on her dead parents.

"My, ain't you a pretty one," he said, slowly kneeling down in front of her. He reached out and touched her with a blood-smeared hand, causing her to back away. "What a sweet toy you'll make."

* * * *

Fifteen-year old Amelia of Egypt sat up in her bed with a scream on the tip of her tongue. Sweat beaded her forehead and her breathing seemed to come in short gasps. "Just a dream," she told herself as she pulled the tangled sheets from her legs, "Only a dream." Yet it was the same dream each year; the nightmare from the night her parents were killed and she had almost been taken.

Amelia got out of her bed slowly. Her room still dark since it was at least two more hours before daybreak. A few more hours before the family had to get themselves ready to travel down to the docks to greet guests and a new member to the family, Alexis Felix of Rome.

An alliance between Rome and Egypt hadn't been made in centuries. The fall out between Cleopatra and Octavian was something still talked about today and the way the Romans took over the country still didn't sit well with some of the people in Egypt now, but with the raids starting up, Egypt needed help.

Things weren't the way they use to be. It would take centuries to rebuild the kingdom to its original glory, and Corydon, her brother, wanted to keep it that way. The country might be more high-tech, more refined, but like so many others the raids that came each year were starting to take its toll on them all.

The raids were getting worse, the death rates growing and the total of guards smaller. Egypt needed help or it was going to die, but the lingering question in Amelia's mind was if her brother, Corydon, was strong enough to do whatever it would take to ensure the country's safety. He was a fair Pharaoh, but not a strong one.

Amelia ran her fingers through her long hair and noticed that her hands were shaking. She'd had the dream before, always the same. The village on fire, people screaming and dying, but it was the first time she ever had it with *him* in it. Amelia stopped dreaming about him a couple years after the death of her parents, so it was nerve racking to have him show up again—the young man who almost took her away after the rape and death of her mother.

She couldn't remember a lot, which was a blessing, but Amelia did know and could never forget that the boy wanted her and that alone had her feeling as frightened as she had been as a little girl.

She rubbed the chill from her bare arms. Her sleeping gown was simple and short, nothing more than a short skirt with a slit up one side and a matching, baggy top that was sleeveless. Amelia had it made short since she tended to toss and turn in her sleep.

Walking on the cool marble with bare feet, she padded to her bathing pool. With the tip of her toe, she tested the water and smiled at the chill. Pulling the cloth from her shoulder to pool at the floor, she walked into the water, enjoying how the coolness chilled her even more and seemed to help ease the nightmare from her mind.

Two fighters were due to arrive today, one to marry her sister, Ismame. Alexis Felix and Drakon Anthony. Rumor had it that Drakon was a blood descendent of the famous Marc Anthony, which she supposed might be true. After all, Marc Anthony did marry and supposedly had children with Cleopatra.

The two were rumored to be favored by the gods with their strength. They were killers, the kind of warriors that Egypt needed if they had any hope of defending themselves from the Drystal.

The Drystal! Vicious people who thrived on killing, raiding, and raping. They took young children for slavery and sold them off to other countries, or they would keep them as sex slaves for themselves. Already over hundreds of children had been taken in the raids in the past few months and the city was about to turn against its Pharaoh for the simple fact that he wasn't protecting his people.

The only thing left for Corydon to do was to hire more warriors to help fight, and even though it took over half of what the palace had in its holdings, it was all they could do. When that didn't work, the next plan of action was to get aid in the one direction others had never thought to look. Rome.

After a long soak to where she was shaking from the cold, Amelia stepped out and wrapped a drying cloth around her body. She pulled on the cord to send for her maid as she sat in front of her vanity, looking at herself.

Amelia had the softest looking green eyes ever, or so she had been told. Her long hair, which reached to the middle of her back, was dark as the night. It also had a slight wave to it, which helped her maid's efforts in curling it for important, lavish ceremonies. Her body was tiny as she stood five-three, petite and slender, reminding some of a young Goddess. She had been told many times over through the years that she was pretty like her mother, but Ismame was the beautiful one in the family and before the raids, the favored to be married to a King of another country. Now the Egyptians were considered to be cursed and no man wanted a cursed bride, because the Drystal kept raiding Egypt, never going to other countries as they had in the past.

Since her hair was thick, it took forever to dry, causing her maid extra work. By the time the sun started rising, Amelia's hair was braided in tiny braids and her headpiece in place on her head.

Long, tiny braids cascaded down her back. The headpiece on her head was nothing fancy. A simple gold band with lapis encrusted around it.

She stood up in order to be dressed by another maid. A sleeveless dress slipped over her head that stopped at her feet. Her gown was made of sheer gold over white, the bodice a black crisscross design over her breasts and wrapped around her waist.

Stepping into her sandals as she headed to the door, Amelia pushed back the dread that washed over her. She couldn't shake her dream, or the vision of the leather boots coming towards her. Amelia wasn't able to recall what the young boy looked like, and was thankful for that, but something told her that her dream was more a memory. If she didn't know better, she would say that the Gods were about to have her meet him again, and that had her shivering in fear.

Ismame and Corydon were already sitting at the long table eating the morning meal when Amelia walked in. Amelia was a bit shocked, thinking that she might be the first since it was so early in the morning, but then again with the excitement of their guests, it wasn't a surprise.

Ismame had the same soft appeal as Amelia, but didn't have her petite frame. Her sister's hair was a darker brown and much thicker. It always curled for her and looked spectacular piled high on her head with one thick curl down the center of her back. She wore the same kind of headpiece as Amelia, but instead of the free flowing dress, she wore a gown with a tight corset with long narrow sleeves and a skirt slit up both sides of her legs.

"Morning." Corydon smiled brightly at Amelia. "Sleep well?"

"Fine." Amelia smiled back, taking her seat to the right of her brother, across from Ismame.

Corydon was nine years older than Ismame, who was only twenty-one but he'd been young when crowned King. He stood at almost six foot two, had a slight curl to his black hair, and the dark brown eyes that were so much like their father. A bronze complexion from many swims and trips to the beaches, firm lips, strong jaw, and he always appeared well groomed. Everything about Corydon was perfection, but for the large scar that ran down the side of his face from when he had saved Amelia from unknown fate.

Corydon dressed in breeches made of the finest black leather. His top was made of thin dark blue cotton that hung loosely on his shoulders and opened halfway down his chest with large gold encrusted buttons. Around his hips, he also wore a belt of gold, which carried the sword adorned with the family crest. At times, Amelia got the impression of a pirate when she looked at her brother.

"I've news that our guests should be here within the hour," Corydon told both of them handing a bowl of bread to Amelia. Amelia took it but Corydon grabbed her arm stopping her from taking a piece. "You had the nightmare again."

It was a statement, not a question. Amelia nodded. "Yes," she answered faintly.

Corydon took the bowl, put it back on the table, and picked up her hand. He brought it up to his lips for a quick kiss. "I wish to this day you didn't have to witness that," he whispered.

Amelia smiled at him, "They're only dreams. I'm only worried about this meeting." She took some bread and turned her attention to Ismame. "Excited?"

"About as much as I can be," Ismame answered. Ismame gave her full attention to Corydon. "I still don't understand why I must marry this Roman."

Corydon sighed aloud. Then he dropped his hand heavily on the table where it landed with a thump, causing Amelia to jump, startled as she watched the exchange between brother and sister.

"Because I said so for one, and second we need the arm of Rome," Corydon stated between his teeth but finished with a yell when Ismame stood up quickly from the table, ready to leave. "Ismame, come back here!"

Since Corydon had informed them of the arranged marriage between Ismame and a Roman, fights broke out constantly between them. While Corydon went off to have it out yet again with Ismame, Amelia stayed seated, after her morning meal and went about her business. In two days, she would turn sixteen and she couldn't wait.

Sixteen was to be a golden year and time for her. Almost like a coming out of sorts. She couldn't wait to get rid of the simple dresses she wore and put on the corset ones that Ismame wore.

At high noon, their Roman guests showed up. Amelia stood outside, on the top steps to the Palace on the right of her brother, Ismame to the left. The sun shined brightly, the chill of the morning air gone and the heat of the day quickly rising. A breeze from the south helped the air from turning dry and the excitement that Amelia felt became hard to contain.

For respect to the ancient ways, carriages came with all of the heavy equipment and wedding party, ten in all.

"So everything for their quarters is ready?" Corydon asked for about the tenth time that morning, breaking the silence and tension.

Ismame answered him in a tight voice, "Yes. I have overseen their rooms personally. Each has servants to attend their needs and pleasures."

Corydon nodded. "Good. I want them to be comfortable as we talk business." He turned to Amelia. "Has the hunting trip been arranged?

"Yes and a feast afterward," Amelia answered with a smile.

She tried to keep up the happy mood and all, but inside, her mind kept racing back to the dream. It always happened right before her birthday, since that was when the raid happened.

Amelia hid what happened the night their parents died. She didn't tell her brother, who was the one to save her from the hands of the killer who'd raped then killed their mother. The things they did to the Queen of Egypt as they took their pleasure haunted Amelia for years.

She had hid in a large pile of hay, as the leader of the raiders pulled her mother from her husband's dying arms. Amelia was in shock when the youth in the leather boots shoved her mother down to the ground, raped then stabbed her to death. When he was finished, and after he put his sword to her, Amelia came out of her hiding place to cry over her dying mother. It was then that he had turned at the sounds of her crying and almost had his hands on her when Corydon arrived. The two fought, each leaving with a reminder of the fight. Corydon sported a scar, leaving his face marred for life as did the youth, who violated not only her home but their mother as well.

Shaking her head, Amelia pushed the memories aside again and watched as the first man came out of the carriage sent to pick them up from the landing platform.

"Alexis!" Corydon called out with a smile on his face, walking down the stone steps to meet the man. The two men clasped each other's arms above the elbow in a jester of friendship. "It is good to see you my friend."

Alexis Felix stood at six foot two and was built like a god. His hair was trimmed at least three inches from his shoulders and blew in the wind. It was a nice shade of sandy blonde that made any girl itch to run her hands through. His eyes were baby blue, his arms t hick and thighs powerfully built with muscle. The leather breeches molded to each muscle, as did the leather upon his feet. Even his crisp shirt, which hung loose, managed to show to advantage his well-honed, muscular body.

"Corydon." Alexis smiled back. "Been too long."

"How was the trip?" Corydon inquired.

"It was great. Uneventful, thank the gods. You should think about having a closer landing strip. The carriage ride almost did me in."

"That was my father's thing. He wanted our city to be as much like our forefathers as he could make it, yet some things even he could not stop." Corydon put his arm around Alexis's shoulders. "Come. Meet my sisters and your bride to be."

Together, they walked back up the steps and stopped in front of Ismame. Amelia only heard half of what was being said between them. She watched them of course, but moved away.

"Like a thief in the night, she slid away into the shadows, where no one would find her."

Amelia turned; eyes wide open, staring at a strange man behind her. She hadn't heard him come up the steps. "But a very pretty young shadow," he added with a smile, then bowing slightly. "Drakon Anthony, at your service."

"Corydon, my right hand man, Drakon Anthony," Alexis said. "He's as good as me with the blade but more sly with the ladies. Come, Drakon, meet my soon to be bride."

Drakon gave Amelia a slight nod before joining Alexis and Amelia watched him go. He stood somewhat taller than Alexis, with tight black leather breeches, leather boots, and a matching black leather vest. His hair, which was also black, touched his shoulders and when the wind blew, those locks went into his dark brown eyes. He glanced back at Amelia again, smiled, and gave her a quick wink before he ran one hand into his hair, brushing it from his eyes.

"Let us get you all settled in," Corydon said. "I'm sure you'd like to freshen up after that trip."

They rested and then, later, joined everyone in the great hall for a feast. Four different kinds of meat lined the long table, as did breads, fruits, wine, beer, and other things to eat. Alexis took Amelia's seat across from Ismame and Amelia was forced to sit in the middle of the table across from Drakon. The wedding had to happen quickly, so the three were discussing the event.

"Alexis told me that you like to race horses," Drakon suddenly said, once again brushing his hair back from his eyes. "Stallions, in fact."

Amelia jumped when he spoke, mostly because she wasn't expecting him to speak to her at all. For as long as she could remember, all the attention went to Ismame, not her. Having him give her some of his undivided attention was a bit strange. "Yes," she answered, picking up her wine glass and taking a sip to calm her nerves. "The best in the galactic."

Drakon leaned back in his seat, stretching his legs out under the table. His foot touched hers and again she jumped, but he didn't move back or act like he noticed. "Is that a fact? Might have to test that one." His eyes seemed to light up. "I'm always interested in horses. Would love to be able to race them myself, but I travel so much."

"When do you think the wedding will happen?"

Drakon glanced down at the table, "They need the strength of both countries to fight the Drystals." He looked at her. "I'm going to take a guess and say within the next couple of days." Her heart sank and it must've shown on her face. "What's wrong?"

Amelia shook her head. "Nothing. Excuse me." Pushing away from the table, she stood up and left the feast, not looking at the guests, but knowing they were all looking at her.

She should have known. Her sixteenth birthday and Ismame would be getting married on it. Hell, she'd bet Corydon even forgot all about it, never thinking once that there might be something else to celebrate besides the wedding.

Yet, the wedding was very important. They needed it in order to survive. Kurel is a powerful land with powerful people. Men used to getting what they wanted and taking it if they had to. She'd seen it first hand, knew of their power.

Amelia walked out to the gardens. She bent over, picked a lotus flower. She brushed her face with it as she strolled; thinking about what would happen after Ismame marries Alexis.

Laughter interrupted her thoughts. Finding a place to hide, Amelia pressed herself into the dark shadows of the night, waiting.

Ismame came out with Alexis. She smiled, teased, and flirted with him. She stayed silent, momentarily watched the two of them interact, but then turned and walked away. She headed back to the palace, back to her childish room and her childish life.

Sixteen was to be her year of coming out, guessing it now had to wait.

* * * *

Drakon lounged on a large golden sofa at the foot of the bed in Alexi's room, waiting for him. In his hand, a large silver cup was filled with sweet wine. He had one leg hanging over the side of the arm, the other on the ground and his head rested on some very nice soft pillows.

Swirling the drink around in the cup, Drakon thought about the young girl, Amelia. Almost a woman, yet not quite. Fifteen if he had to make a guess, or maybe sixteen. Once she finished growing up she would be a knock out, the kind of women that held mystery in her eyes, temptation in her body and could capture your soul with a smile. He almost felt sorry for the poor bastard that claimed her for his own, he thought with a smile.

"What the hell are you smiling about?" Alexis demanded with a smile on his lips, but his brow furrowed.

"Finished already?" Drakon asked. "I figured you'd be out there all night with your bride."

Alexis snorted, removed his dinner jacket, and tossed it to the side. "So what'd you say to young Amelia to have her rushing out?"

"She asked about the wedding. I told her when and she just walked away."

Alexis frowned even more. "Strange." He went over to the table with the wine, pouring himself a large cup before taking a seat across from where Drakon lounged. "Sort of figured it might be that playboy charm of yours. It really is a turn off."

Drakon laughed. "Your last mistress didn't seem to mind it."

"Oh, that's low."

Drakon laughed a bit more then turned serious, sitting up. "So you're really going to go through with this then?"

Alexis nodded, "The Government has requested it. Egypt and Rome need to join forces this time. Together we are powerful."

"Agreed," Drakon nodded, bending over his legs with arms resting on his knees, head down. "I just don't want you to think later on this might be a mistake." He raised his eyes to look at Alexi. "And think you've married the wrong one."

Alexis raised his head up more, eyes locked with Drakon. "Amelia is a lovely young lady, but still a child. This treaty needs to happen now, but will you do it? Will you marry for peace?"

Drakon thought about that. He lowered his head again, staring down at the floor. "I have no home any longer. But if I had, then yes, I would."

His home had been destroyed, like so many others in the raids with the Drystals. He was away, learning the skill of a blade and how to fight. At age eighteen, Drakon came home to nothing. Everything and everyone he loved was gone, making him the sole survivor of his household name. The only thing he had left was his fighting arm, and he made a damn good living with it in Rome. Hooking up with Alexis was one of the best things he did back then and he may have the means to have a home once more, but fighting this war prevented him from building one.

"I always knew that you were the one to marry for peace." Drakon nodded, stood up, and stretched. "We all need this. Only with the combined forces can we defeat our enemy."

"And what would give you peace?"

Drakon thought about that for a few seconds. "To run my blade through the bastard's heart that killed my parents."

"And you shall have it," Alexis stated in all seriousness. "I promise."

Drakon left with a nod, went back to his own room, and headed right for the balcony. The night was warm, but not so warm to make one miserable. He stared out into the night-lights, amazed at how this culture was to return to the roots of their people and recreated the monuments from the past.

New pyramids, a new sphinx, and temples just like the ones from so many years ago. It rather looked like they were in the past and the beauty of it stole his breath away.

"The new Egypt." Drakon dropped his cup, swung around with hand on his dagger at his hip. Amelia stood in his room, her wide; frighten green eyes staring at him in shock. "I'm sorry. I didn't mean to scare you."

Drakon let out a sigh, "It's alright. I should've heard you come in. The city's beauty it seems has distracted me."

She blushed, head lowered and she joined him outside. "The new sphinx was built in seventy-twenty-four. They build it from the old pictures of the original one."

Drakon looked in the direction she pointed. He could make out the large head of the sphinx eliminated by a light shining directly on it.

"I'm sorry for walking out at dinner tonight," she added. "It was rude of me."

"I'm sure all the wedding planning is taking its toll on you also."

She shook her head. "No, it isn't that."

She had a dreamy expression on her face. Amelia leaned forward, against the iron railing, staring out at the city. Drakon found himself doing the same thing.

"My birthday is on the same day as the wedding," she said after some time passed. "I'll be sixteen and no one will remember." Her voice lowered, trailed off, but Drakon heard it all and understood.

"I'm sure your family will remember it."

She smiled, head lowered and body pushed away from the railing. Taking a deep breath, she turned and nodded. "I just wanted to come and apologize and say good night."

Drakon nodded, watched, with growing longing in his eyes, at the beautiful young woman leaving his room.

* * * *

Two days later the city was ready for the wedding.

The festival of marriage in honor of Ismame of Egypt and Alexis Felix began very early. Fish cooked in many different ways was available along with several pigs for roasting over three large pits. There were two cows, also cooked over an open fire for the first time in many years. The great doors to the hall were open for the whole city to offer good wishes to the bride and groom.

Tables lined the walls with bench seats around the cook pits. Music played in the corners of the room and the wine flowed freely. Fruit from every tree graced the tables, fresh bread of every kind, olives, beans, many different types of cheeses and even squid, shellfish, lobsters, and crab was served.

Everyone in the city contributed to the mighty meal and, in doing so, they were allowed and expected to share in the meal at one of the tables. People were having a great time, except for Amelia.

As the feast took place and the whole city were enjoying the wedding celebration, Ismame and Alexis were making their pledges to each other. No birthday congratulations were mentioned to Amelia.

Ismame wore a white corset with long flowing white skirt. To show everyone that she was indeed pure, no jewelry touched her skin. Amelia also dressed in a corset that had wide straps slightly off the shoulders and a long skirt. Her hair was piled high on top of her head with large ringlets skimming on her shoulders. Unlike her sister, Amelia was able to wear jewelry, she just didn't touch the pieces she had on her vanity table.

"Is it that hard of a pick?" Amelia looked up in the mirror and saw Drakon in the doorway, leaning on a statue of Anubis.

Drakon was dressed in black. Black leather pants hugged his legs, black boots reached his knees and a black long sleeved shirt was open at his throat. His hair was brushed back out of his eyes, but one long lock of hair seemed to find one eye no matter what he did.

Amelia's mouth went dry. At sixteen, she saw the man she wanted and it shocked the hell out of her, but she also saw in his eyes what so many others, that passed through the city; Drakon looked upon her as a child.

He pushed away from the statue, strolled up behind her, and bent down so that he could look at her face in the mirror. Amelia watched him reach into his shirt and withdraw a necklace. A wide gold chain held triple circle pendants, the middle of the largest of the three, together. He lowered it down the front of her, clasped it behind her neck and rested his hands on her shoulders.

"Now you're ready." He extended one hand to her. "Shall we?" Amelia took his hand, rose to her feet and let him lead her from the chamber out to the party.

People danced, music played loudly and the wine and beer flowed freely. The wedding was simple, the party lavish. Halfway into the night, the bride and groom left, and Amelia slipped away. She couldn't shake the depressed feelings running through her, even thought she was very happy for the union between Egypt and Rome.

"A happy birthday should be said at least once tonight." Drakon walked out of the darkness, two glasses of wine in his hands. He handed one to her.

"Baby sitting must be very boring by now," she stated, taking the glass.

"Who ever said I was babysitting?" He smiled.

Amelia lowered her eyes, turned, and moved away from him, "It's what you've been doing since you came here. Keeping the child happy so she doesn't throw a tantrum."

"I don't see a child, I see a young lady about to cross over into womanhood." She stopped, turned back around and he took two steps closer. "I've been in your shoes at one time. The youngest, forgotten, but never misunderstand that family is everything. What they forget today, I'm sure will be made up later."

"Because the treaty is so important."

"Without it we cannot enjoy the party within." He took hold of her chin, bringing her face up. "Enjoy your youth, the freedom your sister and Alexis are giving up. Without it you won't have another birthday to be depressed about." His face moved closer to her and she held her breath. "Happy sweet sixteen birthday, Amelia of Egypt." His lips touched hers and the world stopped. It wasn't the kind of kiss she'd seen before, or the kind she'd heard about, but it was a kiss, nevertheless and it happened to be her first.

Amelia sucked in her breath, opened her lips for more, only to have him pull away. She didn't notice she'd closed her eyes until she had to force them open and look at the man who just gave her the first kiss of her life.

Drakon pulled away and she licked her lips. He smiled, turned and walked back inside to the party. Amelia watched him, frowning at his sudden departure. Her heart light, pounding in her chest while she tried to make scene of what just happened. She almost smiled until she saw Drakon wrap his arm around a woman, whisper something into her ear, and walk out of the room with her laughing on his arm.

The party lasted all throughout the night. Come morning, Amelia heard that Alexis needed to go back to Rome, marry Ismame in their culture and then the planning of the strategy to fight the Drystals would begin.

Amelia didn't join Corydon with the good wishes and farewells to the guests. She stayed in her room, watching from the window.

She soon discovered that Drakon had taken his pleasure with the woman last night. From the talk of the servants the next morning, she picked up that he was not only a great lover but also one that didn't leave a partner unsatisfied.

So why did he kiss her? Amelia couldn't answer that question, but she did know one thing. Next time they came face to face, she was going to ask him that very question.

Chapter One

Five years later

"In five years, Egypt hasn't changed that much." Drakon raised his hand up to the bright sky, shielding his eyes as he squinted. "Still bright and hot as hell."

"Well, I for one am happy to be back." Ismame Felix, with a round belly, stepped from the shuttle with a dirty look directed at Drakon.

"As we all know very well," Drakon mumbled under his breath, pushing away from the shuttle to help with the unloading of bags.

For the past few days since they started to put together this trip back to Egypt, all Ismame had done was start to complain about Rome. Too cold in the winters, not enough heat in the summers. She wanted the baby to be born in her homeland, not in Rome. It was enough to have Drakon wanting to ship her ass back to Egypt himself. All she seemed to do was complain about everything.

"You know, I didn't think you were looking forward to seeing your brother and sister," Drakon stated. "My mistake."

"I hear Amelia has turned out to be a very lovely lady." Alexis came out of the shuttle with bags in his hands.

"Didn't Corydon mention he's had many offers for her, but she's turned them all down?" Drakon added, loving how Ismame chewed the inside of her lips with irritation.

Shortly after they left Egypt, he learned of a hidden jealousy between the sisters, or mostly with Ismame and Drakon enjoyed poking at Ismame about Amelia every chance he could get.

Right when the last bag came out of the shuttle, the carriage showed up. As they had five years earlier, their trip into town was made the old-fashioned way. It took another couple of hours to load everything up before they got into the carriages and headed for the city.

Drakon enjoyed the scenery. He looked out the window, closed his eyes when the breeze hit, sank back against the seat. It had been months since he had been able to relax. The fighting had begun to take its toll on him, just like the stress of working out some kind of peace between Drystal and Rome.

Lander Drystal, king of Kurel, wanted peace. He was tired of fighting, the killing, and raiding, but he also was an old man now. His son, Kyril, seemed to be the one Drakon worried about the most. After looking into things more closely, Drakon discovered that father and son were the two Amelia saw kill her parents.

Rome wanted peace. A family was picked, their daughter married to one of the royal family, a niece of Lander, and the fighting between Kurel and Roma stopped, but not for Egypt. No, there was still something in Egypt that Drystal wanted; only Drakon didn't know what the hell it was—yet.

Two hours later, they finally pulled up to the front steps of the Palace. Drakon had a very hard time hiding the smile on his face at Ismame's look of disappointment. Since being informed about the trip to Egypt, she had started to act as if the whole country would be waiting for her return. Now, only servants awaited them.

"Evening." One bowed. "I am instructed to inform you of the celebration of Amelia's twenty-first birthday being celebrated currently. Lord Corydon is most anxious to see you all. Please follow me."

"Twenty-first, huh," Drakon remarked. "To me she'll still be that kid waiting for a happy birthday from her family," he said, following Ismame and the servant into the palace.

The great hall was filled with music and people. For sure, a party was in full swing and Drakon smiled. Sure as shit beat the last birthday, she had.

Right off, Corydon found them. Dressed like a king in black leather pants, white shirt and a cloak, he pushed through the crowd and greeted them with a big smile, arms opened wide.

"Ismame!" Corydon cried out, gaining the guest's attention. "Oh, dear sister, look at you!" The embrace was short, but Ismame's smile was big. "Alexis, Drakon. Welcome!'

Drakon took the hand offered him. He was just about to ask after Amelia when she caught his eye, and immediately, Drakon gave her his full attention.

Amelia strolled behind a long line of people; her head turned to him, meeting him stare for stare. The outfit she wore sure as shit didn't scream childish.

A tight gold corset fitted around her like a second skin, pushing her breasts up, revealing a nice amount of cleavage. The skirt—oh boy! Was it even a skirt? A long matching golden, half skirt connected to the corset and ran down to the floor on one side. The other side was bare as the day she was born. Jeweled bands wrapped around her thigh, then an inch below the knee, calf and ankle. They sparkled when she walked. Her hair was wrapped up at the back of her head, a matching gold and jeweled crown rested on top. Her eyes were outlined in black with the lines going up on each side of her face like the ancient Egyptians use to do. Her arms and wrists were adorned with jeweled bands. She carried a long fur wrap in pure white that dragged behind her. Even the heels she wore had a sparkle to them.

"That is definitely not a kid," Alexis stated from behind Drakon.

"Not one I remember," Drakon mumbled, unable to tear his eyes from the vision before him.

"Amelia, come!" Corydon called out.

She turned, headed right for them. Drakon almost forgot to breath and had trouble swallowing. No way in hell could he tear his eyes off the girl he remembered from so long ago. Five years ago, Amelia was a pretty thing but he also knew she'd be a heart stopper once she finished growing up. Nothing could've prepared him for what stood before him now.

"Congratulation, Ismame," Amelia said. Even her voice had a certain sex appeal to it. "When Corydon told me you wanted to come home for the birth of your child I have to admit, I was a bit shocked."

"Afraid I'd once more take up the light."

Amelia cast Drakon a quick look before facing Ismame again. "No. Just shocked you would want to make the trip in such delicate condition. After all, carrying a child to full term hasn't been an easy thing for you."

"They act as if they haven't been apart for five years," Alexis chuckled.

"Excuse me." Amelia turned and walked away.

Like a damn lap dog with his tongue out, Drakon had to follow her. He couldn't help himself. "You've changed."

"Have I?' she didn't even look at him when she spoke. Then she stopped. "You finished yet?"

"With what?"

Slowly she turned around, and that strange breathless feeling overwhelmed him again. "With checking out my ass."

Drakon laughed. He couldn't help it. "You have changed."

"So some say." Again, she turned and walked away. Drakon followed. He almost bumped into her when she stopped suddenly beside a long table. Turning around she handed him a drink. "So how's living with my sister been?"

Drakon took the cup, watched her take a drink before doing the same. "A challenge."

"I told my brother that Alexis would never be happy with her."

Drakon cocked his head to one side. "And you think he would've been happy with you?" He almost didn't want to hear the answer to it. After he got back home, he heard a rumor that Amelia might've wanted Alexis also. Now, thinking about it, his gut turned.

"That is something neither one of us will ever know." She cocked her head with a slight bow. "Excuse me. I have other guests I must see to."

Drakon let her go, watched each step she took.

"The girl has grown up," Alexis came up behind him and hung one arm over his shoulders.

"She certainly has," Drakon agreed, not able to tear his eyes away from her just yet.

"Careful, my friend." Alexis lowered his voice, leaned into Drakon's back. "That one might get your heart."

Drakon glanced at Alexis and snorted before turning away and heading for the stairs to his room. What Alexis didn't know, was that

Drakon was pretty damn sure she already had his heart.

A hot bath awaited him and a bed he couldn't wait to stretch out on. He was tired, ready to relax and thought he might need all the help he could get at facing Amelia. *What a vision!*

The moment his head touched the silk pillows and the cool sheet landed on his body, sleep took him. He sighed in bliss, letting the music below lull him into a peaceful slumber.

His warrior senses had Drakon waking and sitting up in bed with his dagger in hand. Amelia stood at the foot of the bed, her clothing changed; looking more tempting then she had a right to. Everything downstairs was quiet and the room dark except for the faint light from the swinging oil lamps left to burn through the night.

Her long hair curled down her back in tight ringlets, held back by a band of silver pushed into her hair. A long, loose blue gown adorned with criss-crossed trim encircled her breasts and pearls hung long around her neck. Simple, yet very sexy.

"What are you doing here?" he asked, putting the dagger down, making sure the sheet covered him.

"You left," she stated, bending over and picking up the pants he left on the floor. "We really didn't get to talk much, with the party going on and all."

She tossed him his pants. Drakon caught them, raised one eyebrow and with a sigh she turned around. Once she did, he quickly slid them up his legs and tossed the sheet to the side before getting out of bed.

"You were busy," he said.

"True." When he looked up, she was watching him dress.

"You really shouldn't be in here this late," he told her. "Might ruin your reputation."

She smiled and it just about brought him to his knees. Slowly, Amelia came closer to him, and Drakon couldn't still his pounding heart. "I don't think I have to fear that. Everyone is sleeping." Her chin went up and her eyes sparkled as she stared up at him. She stood so close he could feel her body heat.

"Didn't Corydon teach you manners when I was away?"
"You afraid of me?" she purred, that teasing smile of hers driving him nuts.

"Now why would I be afraid of you?"

"You didn't kiss me hello."

Oh, shit! Clearing his throat, Drakon moved away from her, putting some much needed distance between them, without making it seem like he was doing just that.

"And if my memory serves me right, you did kiss me on my sixteenth birthday." She strolled up to him again, and this time Drakon didn't back away. "I'm older now."

"Are you trying to tell me that no one has kissed you in five years?" One eyebrow went up while he looked down at her.

Those green eyes seemed to sparkle then. "A couple maybe."

"Are you trying to flirt with me?" He grinned, crossing his arms over his chest.

This time it was her turn to move away from him. "The king of Drystal wants peace. Did you know that?"

"I've heard. Recently he made peace with Rome."

"Yes, he has." She swung back around, her long gown flowing around her. "Why did you kiss me back then and left me to go to another's bed?"

"Every girl should have her first kiss on her sixteenth birthday."

"How do you know it was my first?"she said, her eyes sparkling.

Drakon smiled, moved towards her this time. "Oh, I have enough experience to know it was the first kiss." She touched his chest and Drakon stilled. He looked down at the hand. "Don't play games, Amelia," he breathed out, meeting her eyes. "I'm not the kind of man to play them."

"Are you sure about that?" Her hand went up his bare chest, around to the back of his neck, pulling him down to her.

The moment their lips touched, Drakon became lost in the moment. He wrapped his arms around her, slid his hands up her back to her shoulders, pulling her closer.

This time the kiss wasn't anything sweet, light, or innocent. He devoured her with his mouth, took what she offered and sipped at the sweet taste, which belonged to only her.

Gentleness went right out the door. Hunger replaced common sense. Drakon walked her backward until they bumped into the wall. There he slid a hand down, took hold of a leg and had it up to his waist, hand under the skirt. He ground his hardness into her, moaned at the sweet torture her soft body and still it wasn't enough.

He broke the kiss off, pulled at her hair until her head went back, throat exposed. Drakon grazed his lips and teeth from her shoulder up to her ear. She shivered in his arms and he just moved down to the other side, sucking, licking, tasting her flesh, never stopping the rotation of his aching cock to her silk covered pussy.

Back up to her lips, Drakon kissed deep, plunging his tongue into her mouth. He moved his mouth over hers, his tongue thrusting, stroking hers.

He touched bare skin under the skirt and Amelia moaned into the kiss. Drakon kneaded the flesh, parted the globs, and teased the tiny entrance. Her nails dug into his shoulders. The pain did little to still the ach he carried now between his legs.

Again, he broke the kiss off, licked down her throat, cupped a breast, and squeezed. The nipple hardened for him instantly and Drakon rubbed it with his thumb.

"You are so ripe, young maiden." His voice sounded raw and rough to himself. He removed his hand from her skirt, slid both up her front, cupping her breasts. "I could take you right now, if I wanted." He was breathing fast when he spoke, his cock throbbing to match the pounding in his chest. "I could pluck the fruit that you have guarded well." He brushed his thumbs over her nipples and Amelia sucked her breath in quickly. "But I won't."

He stopped everything. Amelia opened her eyes, blinked several times while he backed away from her, working at controlling his breathing.

"The fruit isn't for your taking," she breathed out. "You take liberties Drakon like a man trying to test fate and the Gods."

Drakon rushed forward, grabbing her by the arms pushing her back into the wall, his body pressing into hers once more. "I take liberties that any *man* would take from a willing woman. Don't play this game, Amelia. I'm not the kind of man who will stand by and allow you to tease."

"Really?" She looked like she might smile at any moment but didn't. "Then this game should be very interesting to play." Before Drakon could stop her, she ducked under his arms and rushed to the door. "Till the morning."

Drakon didn't get a peaceful night's sleep after all. Once Amelia left, he went back to bed but only tossed and turned the rest of the night. His damn dick refused to go down, and as much as he tried to relieve himself, he couldn't get it down.

Every thought, every nerve in his body seemed to be tuned into Amelia. He could still taste her on his lips. Smell her sweet scent in his nose and feel the softness of her body. It drove him nuts. Not since his youth did he want a woman like he wanted one now.

With the first signs of day, he dressed and left his room. Servants walked back and forth down the hallway, assisting people in getting ready for the day. Drakon wondered if Amelia might be ready or if she was still sleeping and dreaming about him.

However, he was a bit shocked to discover her in a large study with Ismame pacing the room while Amelia sat in a chair, book up to her nose. Ismame wore a long flowing dress, the sleeves hanging off her shoulders, hair down, and the roundness of her belly showing clearly.

Amelia wore a dark blue tight, long sleeve top that covered her from neck to breasts, stopping there to reveal her stomach but her legs were covered. The skirt went all the way down to the floor and when Amelia turned in her seat, Drakon saw that the back was open and crisscrossed at the top linking with the skirt on the sides. Her hair had the same tight curls as last night and a thick matching band kept it all from slipping into her face.

"I've heard he looks for a wife," Ismame said. "Is that true?"

"Corydon has," Amelia, answered; her attention still fixed on the book some. "But no luck it seems."

"What about the rumor that the Drystal is seeking peace?"

"I'm not sure."

"Well, surely, Corydon could marry and get the peace that way."

"Maybe you should ask him yourself," Amelia turned the page in her book and Drakon smiled. She really was putting on a show she didn't care Ismame was there or not.

"Amelia, please!" Ismame sighed loudly. "I've been gone for five years. You can at least acknowledge me."

Slowly the book closed and Amelia looked up at Ismame. "And what would you like for me to do, dear sister?" Amelia set the book aside and stood up, her long skirt flowing to the floor. "You come to me to inform me of a rumor of peace between Drystal and Egypt, yet you know that the king no longer has a female to wed, which leaves me. In five years one would think your troubling ways would stop."

"My how you've grown up and become so cold." Ismame crossed her arms over her chest and Drakon just watched the scene.

"I doubt you can call me cold when it seems that you refuse to share the bed with your husband," Amelia tossed back. "I'm surprised at all to even see you with child."

"Alexis isn't the kind of lover I thought him to be." Ismame hung her head and turned away from Amelia.

"Is the babe his?" Drakon stiffened at the question, wondering if he wanted to even hear the answer.

"It's his," Ismame stated. "He came to my chamber drunk one night. I refused him, and he just took," she turned back to Amelia. "I think it was the best night of our marriage. The roughness of a man taking what he wants—well I think you can understand."

"Yes you don't have to spell it out for me."

Drakon figured it might be best to show himself now. "Well I must say, I don't think, Ismame, you've been up this early in a long time." He smiled and shook his head, looking her up and down. "Amelia, Your style of dress is something."

"Yes, but for one so young, she shouldn't show so much skin," Ismame butted in. "One might think she's easy."

"You're up early," Amelia stated, ignoring Ismame.

"Couldn't sleep." Drakon met her eyes. "My mind and body refused to shut down."

"A shame." She turned and walked around the chair she just sat in. "Hope you're not coming down with something."

Drakon worked at not smiling and not taking the bait. Instead, he turned to Ismame. "Alexis still in bed?"

"How would she know?" Amelia answered. "She took a chamber on the other side of the palace."

Amelia picked up her book and strolled out of the room. Drakon tried like hell to not watch her go, but was unable to do so. He kept his eyes upon Amelia until she was gone before turning back to Ismame.

"Do you want him to divorce you?" he snapped.

"Don't put this on me," Ismame shot back. "He brought this upon himself when he fucked *my* servant on my bed."

"Casting stones already?" Drakon sat down in the chair Amelia vacated. "Be careful, your glass house might break."

She huffed, turned, and went over to an open window. A few seconds went by before she spoke again. "I know he blames me for his death."

"Just as you blamed him for hers." Drakon stood back up, slid his hands into his pockets, and waited for Ismame to collect herself. She put a smile on before turning back to him. "You two need to fix this before what's left is gone. They were accidents."

During the first year of their marriage, Ismame bore a daughter. Last year, during a riding lesson, her young daughter fell off her horse and broke her neck. That caused Ismame to go into labor early, bearing a son who died hours after birth. The death of both their children seemed to put this bridge in their marriage, one that kept ripping them further apart instead of drawing them closer together.

True to her words to Amelia, Alexis did get drunk one night. Ismame kicked him out of the bed when she caught him with a servant. Already, Drakon knew of her denying him, which lead to the servant incident. That in turn had her kicking him from the bed altogether. Drakon was away when Alexis contracted him. Hurt, ashamed, he told Drakon about how he got drunk and in a rage of need busted into Ismame's room and forced himself upon her not once but all night long. It seemed to finish the tear in their marriage and a split or divorce apparent, until she became pregnant once more. Now the two only talked or acknowledged each other when others were around, putting on the show that they were still a perfect couple. Drakon knew better.

"Then if there is nothing left, have the babe and leave," Drakon sighed, "I'm sure your brother will keep the peace whether you stay with Alexis or not."

"And then Amelia would be free to swoop down and claim Alexis for herself," Ismame's bitterness towards her sister showed right then. "Surely you've seen how she looks at him. She wants him."

"Now I know you've lost your mind." He turned, only to be stopped by her voice.

"If you think Corydon will let you have her you're mistaken. He'll marry her to the Drystals to save his own sorry skin before thinking of

34

her happiness or anyone else's."

"What makes you think I want anything but her friendship?" He couldn't turn back around to face her. Drakon knew without a doubt his face, his eyes, would show the truth of Ismame's words.

"I'm not stupid, Drakon. I see how she looks at you. Its' the same way she looked at Alexis the first time he showed up here. Once the game with you is over, Amelia will just go away. I may have been gone for five years but I'm not blind."

"Not everything is a game, Ismame." He finally did turn around, to glare at her. "Not everyone plays with people. If you came back here to start trouble with your sister then I'll ship you back to Rome myself."

"My, aren't we the little champion," she sneered.

He said no more. Drakon left the room, walking down the hall as fast as he could. Ismame always irritated him, now she just seemed to piss him off.

"How long have you let my sister call the shots?"

Drakon stopped in the middle of the hallway and Amelia slid out from the shadows. "She moves you around like a paw on a chess board.

"How long were you watching?" he turned his head to the right.

Amelia raised one arm up over her head, leaned her body into it, and boldly scanned his body as he had done to hers earlier. "Long enough." Her other hand she rubbed up and down seductively over her hip before stopping with her hand on it. "I could've warned you and Alexis that this marriage was a mistake, but I didn't think either one of you would listen to me back then."

Drakon gave her his full attention, arms crossed over his chest, "This marriage wasn't about happiness."

Amelia rolled her eyes and walked closer to him. "Each marriage should be about happiness. Each bed enjoyed."

Drakon stared at her closely. "What happened to you?"

"I grew up," she whispered, reaching out, touching his chest, fisting her hand into his shirt.

Amelia walked backwards and Drakon became powerless to stop from following her. She stood mere inches from him.

He reached up and touched her cheek gently. He found that the feel of her silky skin caused him to want to touch much more. To see and to taste the hidden treasures that by rights only her husband would receive.

"Yes you have." He whispered at her, dropping his hand back down to his side. "I shouldn't be touching you." He tried to back away, but she held him tight by the front of his shirt.

"You're right." Her voice lowered, as did his head. "So don't."

The coldness in her voice had him still right before he kissed her

Drakon looked her in the eye and saw something change within her. He took a step back but she said nothing. When enough distance was between them, Amelia turned and walked away. Drakon stood there, frowning, trying to understand what might be going on this time and coming up with no answer.

The morning meal lay out on a long table. Corydon sat at the head of it, Amelia to his right. At the other, end Alexis with Ismame to his left. Drakon took the seat across from Amelia.

Bread, cheeses, fruit, and some meat they served up on their plates. Servants came with wine and Amelia seemed to work at not looking at him. Hot to cold, that was how she presented herself to him it seemed.

"King Drystal has been contacting me with great persistence to end this fighting," Corydon announced once everyone started eating.

"The king might want to, but I doubt his son will give up the fighting," Drakon stated, picking up a chunk of bread and some cheese. "Kyril thrives on the bloodshed."

"That's what I told him." Corydon nodded. "His son won't just stop his ways so easy if we come to an agreement."

"So how are you going to come to terms?" Alexis asked.

"I don't know," Corydon, answered. "I'm hoping you two might be able to help me with this."

Drakon looked at Amelia, "And what say you?"

Amelia turned her full attention to Drakon. Once more, her eyes sparkled with life, and it was then he knew the game she played. A game he cared nothing for.

Teasing wasn't something Drakon was accustomed to playing. Flirting he'd done before with different women and a couple of young girls he'd playfully teased. However, to have one open up to him, kissing him in the manner of which Amelia did, then turn cold just wasn't a game he liked to play. She would tease him to no ends until he could be teased no longer.

"I think the Drystals can go to hell," she said.

Amelia pushed herself away from the table, stood and left. Drakon watched her go, as did the others in the room.

"She's changed," he stated.

"Yes she has." Corydon sighed. "Since you all left five years ago the sweet girl inside became the woman you see now. Almost like a scorned woman of sorts."

Drakon looked at him, "Who scorned her?"

Corydon jerked his jacket and sat up straighter in his chair, "I'm assuming it was you."

"Me?"

"Corydon you don't think Drakon has shamed your house, do you?" Alexis asked.

"Of course not." Corydon smiled at Alexi, but that smile didn't seem to reach his eyes. "I'm only stating that she changed, after her birthday kiss I believe." He turned his face once more to Drakon, the smile slipping away.

Drakon sat back in his chair, crossed his arms over his chest, and narrowed his eyes upon the man. "Okay, yes, I did kiss her on her sixteenth birthday. What about it?"

Drakon didn't have any intentions of challenging Corydon, especially in his own home, but he didn't like the direction of this conversation. He almost got the impression that Corydon might be implying Drakon ruined Amelia by a kiss and some attention.

"Oh now I recall, you had a wedding on her birthday and you ignored her and didn't even acknowledge the occasion." He sat forward. "And if I'm not mistaken, the tradition you all have for that year is very important—crossing from child to woman, ignored by her own brother. Excuse me."

He stood, turned, and walked away, breathing deeply to cool his anger.

Back in his room, slamming the door, Drakon huffed in anger. He went right up to a table, snatched up a bottle of wine and poured a large amount in a glass then gulped some down.

"You really shouldn't be in here," he said in a tight voice, keeping his back to the one he knew was there. "The maiden of the house doesn't need to be caught in a man's chamber." He turned. "Especially after your brother suspects something is going on."

"Are you scared of what Corydon might do, if he finds me here?" Amelia asked him with an innocent voice.

"Don't play this game with me, Amelia," Drakon told her. "Don't put me in the position where I have to fight to not take."

"Games are fun." She moved in his chamber with grace, the long skirt fanning out behind her. "Control is tested."

"Is that what you're doing? Testing my control?" he frowned.

"After you left with that woman, I followed you," she said, walking around the room, touching his things. "I watched you with her." She looked at him then. "Saw the things you did to her, with her. You were the first to kiss me, the first to waken what is hidden inside. Tell me something, if I wasn't who I am, would you have taken me to your bed and done those things to me?"

The air in his lungs rushed out. Drakon finished his drink, turned, and slammed his cup down on the table, keeping his back to her. "No," he stated in a tight voice.

Her hands touched his back and he closed his eyes. Down to his rear, she cupped him, resting her head on his back. "I thought so," she whispered. She pushed away from him but Drakon couldn't look at her. "I realized last night, after you kissed and touched me that it would be all I'll ever get from you." He turned his head, watching her as she walked back to the door. "Guess it's time to find another, to fulfill my dreams."

39

Chapter Two

Drakon busted into Alexis's room, slammed the door closed and leaned back with a groan, closing his eyes. "She is going to be the death of me!"

"You are playing a very dangerous game," Alexis stated. "Corydon is going to castrate you if you touch her."

"I don't understand what the hell is going on here." Drakon shook his head and pushed away from the door. "One minute she's all over me, hot as can be, testing my control to the max, and then the next cold as ice. She teases, and then she doesn't. And I know I need to stay away from her, believe me I know that."

"Then what's the problem?"

Drakon took the cup Alexis offered him and sat down. "I feel something for her. Something I've never felt in my life before."

"Corydon is going to use her to get this peace."

Drakon tightened his grip on the cup. "I know," he said through his teeth, his anger surfacing faster than what he liked. "And I don't like it."
"Neither do I." Alexis also sat down with a sigh.

Drakon drank his wine, thinking about nothing, or trying not to. His body hummed with life and the desire to go find Amelia, but he ignored it. He kept telling himself that nothing good would come out of it if he went down that path.

"So did you talk to Corydon about Ismame?" he asked instead of thinking about his other problem, after all, that's what they came back for in a way.

"Some, yes."

"And?"

"He thinks I'm going to end the marriage and break the treaty we have."

"Are you?"

"I assured Corydon that no matter what our peace treaty is concrete."

"But what are you going to do about her?"

"What are you going to do about Amelia?"

Drakon grimaced. "Not talking about her."

"Drakon, we're going to be here for a while. There's only so much one can run before they get caught."

"She's not running."

"No, but you are. How long do you think you're going to be able to hold out?"

* * * *

Kyril of Drystal stood in his father's throne room as straight as he could, no emotion on his face. The hall was dead, everyone gone but for him and the king. Lander of Drystal. Not a good sigh.

The throne room was a large empty room most of the time. When special feasts were held, the cold stone floors were lined with animal hide rugs and heavy oak table and benches. Thick rugged tapestries hung

41

along the walls to help keep out winter's chill. Burning torches on chains as well as candles gave off light and three large pits in the center of the room burned for warmth. Lander kept his home fashioned in the Stone Age times. He hadn't upgraded a thing, just merely fixed it up. He even required his people to keep with the dress of the old days, but Kyril refused that. He wasn't going to walk around the chilly halls of the stone castle in a damn skirt. He wore his leather pants and loved the silk shirts, soft leather boots and fur lined wraps.

At his side, Kyril wore the family sword, but hidden in his boot on the right leg was the laser pistol of the new generation. He was a dirty fighter, but he learned it all at his father's side. Kyril loved the fighting; the blood, the taking, and he didn't want it to end. He had one last place to take, one that the Drystal's had been trying to take for years. Egypt!

It was the only spot that Kyril and his father couldn't take. They were close once. Kyril was sixteen when they first raided the planet. It was his first real takes of the killing and raping. He lost count quickly at how many died by his sword, but he could still recall his first tasteful rape. She was the queen and his first, but not the last. Once he was finished with her, he slit her throat, watching the life slip from her body, on his father's command. He almost had another for his pleasure, but the girl was saved. Later on Kyril learned it was the brother and prince, now king of the land that saved the girl.

However, Kyril didn't walk away empty handed that night. He came home with a nice scar down the front of his face, a straight scar from his left eyebrow down to his chin. He owed that boy one, and planned to pay him back. In fact, he tried twice before his father called him back. The new king of Egypt made an alliance with Rome. Kyril tested that alliance and discovered that it was very strong. He couldn't take either places, but that didn't mean that he was going to give up either. That is, until his father declared enough.

"I want her, damn-it!" Kyril said at last, feeling like the silence between them went on long enough. His anger boiled over so much so that he wanted to kill, spill blood and hurt something. "And I don't give a damn how either."

"So you've said," Lander, sighed, motioning for one of the slaves to bring him his drink. He coughed softly before taking a drink, motioning for her to leave.

Lander of Drystal was a frail old man that looked too small for the chair he sat on. Kyril looked upon his father with both respect and disquiet. This whole idea for peace was a joke in Kyril's eyes. It wouldn't work, no matter how much the old man wanted it.

"My Lord, a message." A servant came in quickly, knelt down at Lander's feet with a message in hand.

Lander read it and soon the quiet walls echoed in his ageing laughter. He motioned for the servant to leave, and then looked up at Kyril. "Well my son, it appears as if your greatest desire will come true." He wheezed.

"And what might that be?" Kyril asked.

Kyril watched his father from the corner of his eye. The sight of him disgusted Kyril. At one time, his father was a very powerful man and warrior. He hunted, raided, took the best maids to his bed willing and unwilling, and claimed a lot land in his prime. He showed Kyril the right way to rule and the wrong way. Taught him how to not be soft when it came to wanting and taking things. Being nice was being soft and one didn't want to be soft when it came to ruling. Now the years of all that caught up with him, leaving Lander nothing but a soft old man.

Lander struggled to catch his breath. He motioned for Kyril to come closer, which he did. Kyril went down to one knee before him, looking up at the man who taught him everything. However, he went down out of respect of the crown he wore, nothing else. "The young one that slipped from your fingers shall now be yours!" Lander smiled. Being an old man in his eighties, his teeth were still white and straight.

Kyril took the letter from the winkled hand and read it. It was an alliance agreement between Amelia of Egypt and Kyril of Drystal. A marriage contract!

Therefore, the young girl that slipped his fingers has a name!

"You arranged my marriage!" he yelled, standing back up, staring at the words on the paper. "Have you lost your mind?"

"Egypt has the wealth we need, and you must not destroy it. It is a vast empire and yes, worth the weight in gold. If you go in there and strip the land for your own gain, then you won't have a thing in the years to come. I've told you that before." Lander breathed hard and fast, his face getting red as he yelled at Kyril. "I know what you lust for. I lusted for the same thing once, but I will not have a bastard on my thrown!" He strained to talk, more so than normal. It was a sign that his time was getting very close. "I'm sending you to seal this deal. Marry the young maiden and end this war. Her pureness will give you the heir that we need," Lander, panted. "Not a houseful of bastards!"

"I can take Egypt, the wealth and the girl; I don't need a fucking marriage!"

Lander caught him off guard. He slapped Kyril so hard he tasted blood in the inside of his mouth and took a step back. "I have always given you everything you've ever wanted. You're spoiled and rash, but you will remember your place! I'm still king here!"

"Forgive me, Father." Kyril lowered his head, hoping the jester would calm his father down some.

"So greedy you are," Lander huffed, slumping back in his chair. Kyril looked up, frowning at his father. "You want her for that burning lust and I want the gold that will pay off our men and all the debts. A princess such as her should have a nice price on her virtue, don't you agree? Besides, Corydon is a weak king. You shouldn't have any trouble with taking over once you marry her."

"You don't really think peace with them is possible?" Kyril said.

"The king is weak, but not stupid." Lander wiggled a finger in the air. "He has an alliance with Rome. That gives him a slight upper hand, but not even Rome alone has been able to defeat our army. I know you like the fight, but you must also look at things from another angle. We have procured most of the land. Whom will you fight when there is no one left? There comes a time when you do have to sit back, enjoy what you've got and let them rebuild. If you want to knock them back down again."

"So what is it you're commanding, my lord?"

Lander met Kyril's eyes. The cold look sent chills down Landers's spine. "You want this maiden and I want the gold that comes with her. Marry her. That's an order and command form you father and king."

Kyril bit the inside of his cheek before nodding up at his father. They shared the same gray eyes and many other features. When he glanced at his father, Kyril saw the old man that he would become one day.

"I will bring you the stained sheets from her virginity, Father." Kyril bowed his head.

Lander laughed. It was a frail sound in the empty hall. "I have no doubt you will and be visional, Kyril. Don't be swayed by your desire. I want peace, but I always want respect." He put his finger on the paper. "We are promised a maiden for marriage. I don't trust this young king, and neither should you. Learn, discover, and keep your eyes open. Make sure

Kyril stood up. "The maiden will be mine."

Lander nodded, "Then prepare yourself for the journey. I pray to the gods that I live long enough to see your first-born y son. Now go."

* * * *

Ismame went into early labor. Her cries coming from her bedchamber was enough to cause the whole house to worry, mostly because it came so early.

Alexis found Amelia just as she ran down the hall to the chamber. He grabbed her hand, stopping her before she could go inside. "I sent for the doctor." He looked hard at Amelia. "Please take care of her, and bring me the child as soon as it's born."

"Okay," Amelia said.

Amelia rushed in and was shocked to find so many people in Ismame's chamber. Normally giving birth there was only one maid, a doctor and the nurse to tend to the child. What she saw gave her the chills and had warning bells going off.

"Out!" Amelia snapped. "I want this room cleared out but for the doctor and nurses!"

"I want them here!" Ismame cried between the contractions.

"And I don't give a damn what you want." Amelia informed her. "Get the hell out!"

It took ten minutes for the room to clear out, leaving only Amelia the doctor and both nurses. Since this was Ismame's third birth it moved along quickly. Two servants came back to help Ismame with sitting up and pushing. Amelia stayed next to the doctor, waiting and watching.

On the fifth push, Amelia smiled. The crown of a head could be seen. Within minutes, the child was pushed out into the world and the cry it made was music to Amelia's ears.

"What is it?" Ismame asked in a weak voice.

Amelia took the crying bundle from the doctor before the midwife could take it and held it tightly. She smiled as she looked into the face of the baby. "You have beautiful son."

"I want to see."

Amelia held the baby tightly to her breasts as she walked up to her sister. Not bending over too much, and not letting go, she showed the baby to Ismame.

"He should be happy," Ismame said with no emotion in her voice. "Another son, to replace the one he lost."

Amelia stepped back from her sister. She looked at her as if looking at Ismame for the first time. She turned and walked out of the chamber with the baby in her arms. She thought that she would feel guilt over taking the child away and placing him in Alexis' arms and not Ismame's but she didn't.

"Where are you going?" Ismame yelled.

"I am taking Alexis his son." Amelia stopped at the door and looked back at her sister. "As he requested."

Amelia didn't wait to hear what her sister might have said. She quickly left the chamber. Only when the doors closed did she look up at Alexis. "You have a son."

Alexis walked up to Amelia slowly. Amelia saw the love and concern in his eyes. After the loss of a son and daughter one tended to not believe that there could be another to fill that void or take away the sorrow of the lost.

"He is strong?" Alexis whispered. "Did he come too early?"

"He is strong." Amelia handed the baby over with a smile.

Corydon walked up to look at the baby. "He is beautiful."

"A fine son you have there," Drakon remarked with a bright smile. He looked at Amelia who was also still smiling.

"Come." Corydon slapped Alexi on the back. "Let's go and show this fine boy off. Amelia! We celebrate tonight!"

Amelia was still smiling as the two walked off with the baby. Drakon also stayed, grinning at the two.

"You did a good job," Drakon told her. "Alexis deserves this after the pain he's endured."

Amelia looked at Drakon with an odd twinkle in her eye. "I did nothing. Only waited." Drakon took a step closer, only to have her take two back away from him. "I need to get the celebration prepared."

* * * *

He let her go and it hurt to do so. Drakon didn't like the feelings that stirred inside him over Amelia.

A party had been set up for the birth of Alexis Felix's son. The feast was made up of freshly hunted meat, fresh-baked breads among several other foods. The smells of cooking in the kitchen filled every room in the palace.

Drakon stayed with Alexis. He named the child Cornelius and got a good bill of health for the baby, even though he came early. After the baby was cleaned up and dressed, Alexis held him in his arms, pacing his chamber, staring down at him.

"I ordered a nurse for him," Alexis stated softly. "Doctor thinks he shouldn't have any trouble nursing. He's a strong boy."

"You don't trust Ismame?" Drakon asked.

"Right now I only trust you," Alexis said. "Corydon went to town to find a crib for him. He isn't going to leave my sight. We had a fight you know. She told me she was going to leave me and that I'd never see the child and as far as she was concerned the treaty was over. I told her she could leave any time she wanted, but the child would stay with me. She started to scream all kinds of crazy shit. Then the baby came. I think she tried to make herself have a miscarriage, even this late in the pregnancy." He stopped walking and met Drakon in the eye. "I've told Corydon that the marriage is over, but the treaty will stand as long as I have my son. She takes him from me and it's over." Drakon nodded and sighed. "I've even mentioned it to him that it might be a wise thing for him to consider you for an alliance."

"I'm sure that went over well," he smarted off.

"All you have to do is admit what most of us see." He gave Drakon a frown. "So when are you going to finally admit it to me again?"

"Admit what?"

"That there's something between the two of you." Slowly Alexis put the sleeping baby in a temporary bed and turned to meet Drakon's eye. "It shows in your eyes you know."

"Alexis," Drakon sighed again. "I've been gone for five years and yet it feels as if I've never left her." He walked over to the window, stared down at the Nile. "Ismame sees a threat, Corydon a tool. I see a woman who is so lonely that she'll reach out to anyone."

"And you want her."

Drakon looked at Alexis. "And I want her. So damn bad it hurts deep in my soul." He turned back to the river. "But sometimes we can't have what we want."

A knock on the door and it opened, allowing servants to enter, carrying a large wooden cradle. Behind him, Amelia strolled in wearing a gown that stole his breath just like the first time.

When she turned, showing the servants were she wanted the cradle, Drakon saw that her whole back was bare; the dress went low to the top swell of her rear. He wondered for a split second, as he stared his fill, how the hell the thing covered her breasts at all since it was held up by only a collar and bands.

"This is Luna," Amelia stated after all but one servant left. "She is very loyal to me and I trust her."

Luna stood shorter than Amelia did. She dressed in a simple wrap around dress, no jewels, or make-up on her face. "It's a pleasure to serve you and your son."

"She's also been instructed to lock the doors and only open once she hears your word or safe word," Amelia added. "However you wish to do it."

"You didn't have to go to all this trouble," Alexis stated.

"It wasn't any trouble." She smiled at him and didn't look once at Drakon. "The party starts in a couple of hours. I'll see you there." She gave him a nod, turned and walked out.

Drakon followed her.

"Amelia!"

"I don't have time right now."

Drakon caught up with her, took her by the arm, and stopped her. He looked around for a place to talk that might be a bit more private, found one and dragged her in.

"What the hell do you think you're doing?" she demanded, jerking out of his hand.

"From hot to cold. My how you can turn it off."

"You made it very clear you didn't want me, so I'm moving on. Now, if you'll excuse me, I need to make sure things are going as planned. I don't have time to play games, Drakon. Not with someone that isn't interested." She brushed past him, and he let her, stunned.

* * * *

Corydon laid out his finest wine and had one deer roasted honor of his nephew. Amelia ordered other food like fresh bread, fruit, vegetables, and some pastries. The party got into full swing and Drakon noticed as the meal progressed so did Corydon with his drinking. In fact, Drakon lost count of how many drinks the man had and wasn't at all surprised he got shit faced drunk.

"You need a husband," Corydon said in a slurred tone, slamming his fist down on the table, his attention on Amelia. Everyone stopped what they were doing to stare at him. "One that can keep you in line and melt that cold heart of yours."

"This isn't the place to be having this conversation," Amelia said, keeping her eyes from looking at Drakon.

Corydon shook his head and almost fell back when he stood up. "Any place in my house is right for this kind of talk! Kyril will make you a fine husband."

"Kyril! What are you talking about?"

"He's made an offer, one that is worth my time and worthy of you!" he yelled, pointing a finger at her.

Amelia stood up. "Have you forgotten what he did? Have you lost your mind!" she yelled back.

"Marriage to such a man isn't all that bad," Corydon shot back. "He has strength and power and if he will stop using it on us with you as the price then I'll sell you to him without any regret."

"Kyril can go to hell and you can go with him!"

Corydon backhanded Amelia so quickly that Drakon didn't even see it coming. She went down hard, and he quickly moved to her side, helping her sit up.

"Corydon!" he snapped at the man. "What the hell is wrong with you?"

"You will learn your place," Corydon slurred, pointing his finger at Amelia. "In my house you will do as you're told and marry whomever I say."

Amelia shrugged Drakon off and stood up. She had a standoff with her brother, one that made him instantly coming to attention in case a big fight was to break out. "He'll never have me." She turned and rushed out of the room. Drakon faced Corydon, shook his head at the man, and walked away himself.

"Amelia, wait!" he called out once he caught sight of her.

She started running from him, which in turn had him running after her. It didn't take much before he caught her. Grabbing her arm, he stopped and swung her around. Her hand came out and slapped him hard across the face. It was a move he didn't see coming. "Get your hands off of me!"

"Nice right hook."

"You knew, didn't you?" she accused. He saw the anger in her eyes, the hurt, and disbelief laid out for anyone to see.

"No, I didn't."

"Liar!" She shoved hard against his chest and Drakon took a step back. "I don't believe you." She turned her back to him. Drakon wanted nothing more than to reach out, take her into his arms, and ease all the pain. "Do you know what he did?" she whispered.

"I know what he's done in the past."

"I saw him rape and kill my mother." When she turned back around tears were in her eyes, a few fell down. "And my brother wants me to marry him."

"You're scared."

"I'm *not* scared!" she hissed, her chin going up. "I'm disgusted."
Amelia did the most unexpected thing ever. She lunged into his arms, kissing him deep, fisting both hands into his air. Drakon became instantly lost in the kiss. He took two steps forward, pressed her up against the wall, and deepened the kiss even more. He let the pleasure and his lust have what little treasures he could get.

"God, how you tease me," he said in a husky voice, his cock throbbing so painfully he feared there might be damage. "One can get so lost in the simple pleasure of a kiss."

His lips scooped down on hers once more, taking anything she said away. The kiss was intense, hot, and deep and it brought everything he wanted to do to her to the surface. He forced his tongue deep inside her mouth as his lips moved over hers. He tasted the wine she drank for dinner and tasted the innocence that was still there.

Drakon devoured her. He felt like he couldn't get the kiss deep enough, even as he pulled her closer to his body. One hand on her head as the other wrapped around her waist, and still he deepened the kiss. He found that once he started this, he couldn't stop. He wanted more from her. Wanted to feel her cool skin touch his own. To feel the soft curves against his hardness. To take what Corydon so carelessly was trying to give away.

Drakon moaned when her fingers raked his scalp. Nothing felt as good as when she wrapped her arms around him and pressed closer. He felt her need rise and had to fight to keep what little sanity he had in check.

The arm he had around her waist moved. He moved it down and

cupped the curve of her ass, pressing Amelia into the hardness that pounded between his legs. Her sharp intake of air seemed to be the cold water he needed to stop before things went way out of control.

Drakon found that breaking the kiss was the hardest thing he ever had to do. His body screamed at him for more while his brain screamed to back off. Now was not the time or place to give into a whim. To kiss the maiden of the house and to feel her body pressed against his own could bring about his death. Corydon wanted to marry her off for what he hoped and thought would be peace. Drakon wanted her for his own selfish needs.

Breathing hard and working to get his body under some kind of control, Drakon rested his forehead on her. The need for more overwhelmed him, yet he fought it. He kept telling himself that he had to back off and stop before things got way out of hand.

"Now, my Lady," Drakon said in a rough, thick voice. "I suggest you retire to your chamber before things get out of *my* hands."

Amelia rested her face against the crook of his neck. Her lips grazed his neck while her hand slid down the front of his chest. "I do have to agree with you." She kissed his neck, slipping her tongue out to taste the skin. "Things could really get out of hand, if we keep this up." Before Drakon could say or do another thing, Amelia dogged under his arm. She didn't walk away as he had somewhat hoped, but instead only took two backward steps. "And I must admit the idea is very tempting."

Drakon rested his whole body against the cool wall and groaned when she turned and walked away from him. "She is going to be the death of me," he said to himself before he also pushed away from the door and left the chamber.

For the next couple of days it felt as if Amelia worked extra hard at staying away from him. By the end of the week, Corydon announced to them all that he had indeed accepted a contract for the arranged marriage between Amelia and Kyril Drystal. It took him a lot of willpower and control to not beat Corydon to death over this.

A special feast was ordered in honor of Kyril. He was to be there in only one day. Apparently, he-man was in a hurry to marry Amelia, another small thing that pissed Drakon off and had him drinking a bit too much.

"Don't come to the feast."

Drakon looked up from between his legs, on the floor, to Alexis. In his arms, the baby slept deep and peaceful, and in Alexis' eyes was concern.

"Why not?" Drakon asked, tossing the empty cup across the room and standing up.

"Because you'll only cause trouble," Alexis sighed. "I know you care for her, Drakon, but this is out of your hands."

Drakon moved to the open window, looked out, and spotted the approaching carriages that carried things to make Kyril Drystal more comfortable during his stay. Hell from the look of them it seemed like the man was moving in, not just saying for a short amount of time. Man, he hated Kyril more than hate itself. He and his father took everything from him, left him with a name only, and now they wanted peace. Now Kyril wanted one last thing that Drakon wanted for himself most. Amelia.

"He can't have her," Drakon said through his teeth.

"He can if Corydon gives her to him."

"She isn't a fucking tool!" Drakon raised his voice then winced when the babe began to cry. "I'm sorry."

Alexis went over to the door. "Luna!' he called out. The nurse showed up at once and took the baby. "Drakon, you have to stop this. It's an obsession and it's going to get you into trouble."

"Do you fear for what will happen to Egypt and Roma, or me?"
"I'm worried about *you*."

Drakon turned back to watch the carriages. "He'll destroy her."

"Do you love her?"

Drakon didn't give much thought to love. Over the years, he didn't think such a thing existed. True, his parents seemed to care for one another but he doubted very much that they loved each other. Their marriage had been arranged, like so many others around here. True, it might not be the old barbaric times, but marriages for peace became just as common as it did in the old times. When the Drystals began to wage war on everyone, arranged marriages was the way to get the strength one needed to fight them off.

Love. What a strange word to call ones feelings, and yet Drakon felt as if he did love her. Hell, already he knew he couldn't live without her. It hit him so fast five years ago when he first saw her sad eyes. Even then, he knew he couldn't be without her. Over the years, fighting with Alexis all he could think about was her. Shit, he couldn't even bed another woman just because Amelia was all that consumed his mind, his world.

"Yeah," he breathed out. "I love her."

"Then I can't believe what I'm about to say here, but if you do love her then don't let Corydon or Kyril destroy her or make her into a pawn. And if she is yours, then she'll give you all she has."

Drakon once more turned around to face his friend. "What're you saying?"

"I'm saying love her, Drakon. Just love her and let the rest of the pieces fall as they may."

Chapter Three

For two days, Amelia stayed away from Drakon. She had to. Things felt like they were quickly getting so out of control that she wasn't sure if she *could* control him as she first thought. The kisses she loved dearly and enjoyed them immensely but it seemed that every time he touched her, took the liberties that they both knew he shouldn't, she just wanted to melt at his feet. She wanted to give him everything she could and knew it was so wrong to do so. However, on the flip side she would much prefer to give Drakon everything she had of value instead of letting that bastard Kyril have her. Just the thought of him touching her, taking her virtue and whatever he desired gave her the chills, and not in a good way.

By the fourth day, everyone in the kingdom knew of her upcoming marriage to Kyril. Amelia could feel the mixed emotions from everyone and hear the whispers around the palace. Most were confused over Corydon's choice, others a bit angry, and a few happy thinking that the fighting would finally end.

At the end of the week, news came that Kyril had landed and the carriages sent to pick him up.

Amelia sat alone in her room, in front of the vanity table, staring at nothing when Corydon walked into her room without knocking. Behind him her two maids followed, one carrying something across her arms in pale pink the other a medium size box.

"What's going on?" Amelia asked, turning in her seat to face him.

Corydon smiled like a child getting a very special treat. "A present from you husband to be. He sent it days ago with the request that you wear it when he comes. I've been told that his ship has landed and the carriages should have here within the hour."

The maids placed everything on the bed and stood back waiting. Amelia looked at them then back to her brother. "And if I refuse?"

"Come Amelia," he sighed, the good humor in his eyes fading. "Why must you fight what is already in place. The contract has been accepted. This marriage will ensure the safety of our people."

Amelia stood up quickly and he stopped talking. She moved over to the bed, picking up the dress and matching cloak that went with it. "You're out of your mind if you think that this marriage will stop a man like that." She tossed the dress back on the bed carelessly. "Giving me to him will only sate his hunger, not get rid of it."

"Leave us," he ordered her maids. Once they closed the door, Corydon's anger came full blast towards her. He advanced, backing her up to the far wall next to her bathing pool. "Now you listen to me and you listen real good. You will marry Kyril and you will make damn sure he stays happy and stays out of my lands. If you displease him in any way I will beat you within an inch of your life."

Amelia couldn't stop herself from raising her chin, standing her ground. "I don't think I ever thought I'd see you act just like our father."

He snorted and pushed away from her.

Amelia didn't move. "His hunger for power is what started this damn war, did you know that?" Corydon waved his hand at her in a gesture to shut her up. "Mother told me all about it, but I doubt they ever thought to tell you. She was to marry him. Kyril's father." That had Corydon stopping, facing her once more. "She did. She ran out on him the day of her wedding to our father. Those people were the ones who our grandfather wanted to give the land to by our mothers' hand—the only heir to the kingdom and just like you now, willing to sell it away."

He came at her fast and hard, striking her across the cheek, knocking her down. "I never thought my giving you your leave as I have over the years would turn you into a selfish woman. Dress in the gown and be on the steps to greet your husband to be. They'll be no more talk about it. It's done!" He turned and stormed out, leaving her on the floor.

She rose slowly and donned the pink cloak just as a message came stating that Kyril was here. Amelia closed her eyes and willed herself to be strong. Dressed in the gown of his choice she felt more like a possession instead of a person. Felt as if she was being dressed up just for him.

Now under normal circumstance she might enjoy the dress that hugged her body like a second skin. Pale pink and snug-fitting, it went over one shoulder, down the floor and slit up on the opposite side of the shoulder. A thick gold belt with very pale pink gems hugged her waist and gold trim went all the way around the edging of the dress and cloak. A matching crown was placed over her head, her hair was curled but fell loose around her and a hood had been placed over her head on top of the crown. Standing in the middle of her room, staring at her reflection in the mirror is how Corydon found her when he came in to get her.

Without a word, he took her arm and led her outside. They waited on the top steps for the approach of Kyril Drystal's carriage. As she waited, she also felt eyes upon her. Lowering her head but turning it to the left, she glimpsed Drakon standing alone watching her. Just the sight of him had her heart quickening, pulse speeding up. Never in her life did she want to rush to one man before, as she wanted to right this second. She wanted to run to him, have him hold her and make this whole damned nightmare end.

The carriage pulled up to the front marble steps and out came her nightmare in the flesh. Kyril Drystal stood tall and proud. His dark brown hair fanned out around his tanned face, his silk top hung open from the middle of his chest up to his throat, and the leather pants he wore hugged his thick legs like a second skin.

One of the first things that gave her the chills right off was the scar on his right cheek. A flash of the night her mother was killed hit her. She saw clearly, as if it happened only moments ago, Corydon striking Kyril, leaving a gash on his face. That scar alone would always help to remind her of that night.

How am I going to go through with this?

"Kyril!" Corydon called out, smiling big. "Welcome."

She watched the two men grip one another, Kyril also smiling big. His cold dark eyes never did match the smile on his slightly thin lips. The second those eyes moved to her she shivered, whether in disgust or fear she couldn't say.

"My lady." He reached for her hand and Amelia was hesitant to give it to him. A quick glare from Corydon and she slowly gave him her hand. He took it, bent over and kissed it.

"It's a great honor and pleasure to finally be meeting you. Corydon has expressed to me your beauty and I must say he didn't nearly get it right. You are breath taking."

With a jerk to free her hand from his hold she tried to smile, more for Corydon's sake than his or hers. "Thank you."

"Come!" Corydon smiled. "I have a feast just for you and a great hunt planned, but you must want to rest after your journey so let me show you to your rooms."

Amelia stayed put, letting the men walk past her. She didn't need to look over her shoulder to know that Kyril watched her. She could feel his eyes upon her. When she did turn it was to look in the direction she had seen Drakon standing and watching. He wasn't there now. Feeling the need to get away, she turned and headed back inside to her own chamber. Once there she changed her clothing, dressed in a white pair of spandex jumper suit for riding with a matching fur wrap that went all the way around her from the waist up. Fur boots on her feet and she was dashing out of the palace as fast as her feet could carry her.

She rode away fast and hard, feeling the breeze hit her face, feeling a small sense of freedom in the ride. However, her ride came up short when she spotted Alexis sitting on his mount, staring out at the sands alone. Pulling her own mount into a walk, she went over to him, wondering what brought him out as well.

"Alexis," she breathed. "What brings you about?"

He turned and instantly smiled at her, "Amelia. I sort of figured you would be with your new guest."

She snorted, "As if I wish him to be here." Turning her head in the direction that Alexis happened to be staring at she frowned. "Is that Drakon?"

"Yes."

"What's he doing?"

"Hunting. It helps to clear his mind and calm him down."

She turned her frown to him, "Clam him down? What's wrong with him?"

"Well I'm going to take a guess here and say it's you." He met her eyes and it took a lot of control on her part to not look away. "There's something about a man who fancies a woman, Amelia, and what I mean by fancies is desires her above all else and others. He becomes a stranger to everyone around him and lost to his own wants and needs."

"I don't understand."

"Don't you?"

She shook her head.

"In all my years of knowing Drakon, I've seen him show great restraint when it came to a woman he wanted. I'm not going to lie to you sister. He wants you, and he honors you with great respect. He hasn't claimed you for his own."

"You make it sound as if I'm some prize."

"To the one that holds our hearts, a woman is." She looked back at Drakon off in the distance. She could barely make him out as he walked deeper into the trees for his hunt. "He's been drinking, and that's something Drakon never does."

"There is not much one can say when a man drinks his pain away," Amelia stated, keeping her eyes on the shadows she could see. "I hear it caused one to seek out anything that will spread for him."

"True," Alexis chuckled with a sigh. "And it can cloud one's judgment. I don't like to see him hurt like this and yet I'm powerless to help him."

"How's Ismame?" She needed to change the subject, needed to get her mind off Drakon and Kyril. Hell, she just needed to get away from it all.

"Depressed." Alexis sighed again, this time sounding hurt himself. "I took the babe to her this morning and she didn't even want to look at him or me. She had been depressed from the birth of our first child, but this one is worse. I've sent for the doctor to come and look at her."

"How is Cornelius doing then?"

"Growing." That had him smiling again. "Luna assures me that for a child born early he is very strong, has a nice appetite. I keep him with me at night."

"And how long are you going to stay?"

Once more, he looked out at where Drakon hid for the hunt. "I had planned on leaving once the baby is strong enough to make the trip, but I have a gut feeling that Drakon won't leave just yet. It also doesn't help things that Ismame isn't doing well." He looked back at her. "She isn't eating either."

"I'm sorry Alexis."

He gave her a short smile. "Don't worry about me. You need to focus on you for a change."

It was Amelia's turn to take the deep breath, letting it out slowly. "I don't think my fate is good as long as my brother insists on this marriage."

"Don't give up on hope. I'm sure there is a way out of this. We all just have to think about it, but let me give you one bit of advice. Something I hope you will keep in mind from this moment on."

"And what might that be?"

"Don't play with fire, Amelia. You'll only get burned and I don't wish for you to be hurt more than what you already have."

He nudged the horse to move forward and she was going to let him go, but one nagging question she had been carrying around for so long begged to be asked. "Do you regret going for her hand and not mine?"

Alexis stopped and turned in his seat. She held her breath, waiting for the answer and feared for a moment that she might not get it when he looked back toward Drakon. "As much as I should, I don't. The gods have sealed my fate, yours they have not. You were never meant to be mine, but another's." With that said, Alexis took off in the direction of Drakon, leaving her alone.

A large feast, as large as Ismame's marriage feast, was planned. Amelia was expected to dress as glamorous and as sexy as she had for her twenty-first party.

She didn't.

Instead, she dressed as a maiden of the house in all white and silver. A flowing silk gown of the purest white hugged her body, a thick silver belt around her waist. Her hair was curled at the ends, parted in the middle, and hung down her back in shiny waves with a silver band crown over her head. Since the dress also had a high slit on the side up to her waist, she choose silver heels with diamonds encrusted in the leather with straps that reached from ankle to thigh.

Word came that Alexis decided to have his meal with Ismame. Drakon would be joining them and representing Rome in Alexis' place. That had Amelia dreading the meal even more.

When she entered the room all talking stopped. Kyril stood next to Corydon, dressed in leather pants, a silk top and sword at his side. His hair still had a bit of dampness from a bath and she could read the lust in his eyes. Drakon stood off to the side, drinking. He gave her a quick glance before turning his back on her, which pissed her off.

Normally, since this was her party as well, she would go and join Kyril and her brother first, but the way Drakon acted sparked something deep inside her that she just couldn't ignore. She turned and walked right over to him, ignoring the gasping in the room and the whispers of the staff as she made her way.

"If you're going to stand around drinking like that, thinking that whatever it is you might feel will go away, then just go to the damn barn and drink. I don't want to see you at my party drunk on your ass."

His shoulders stiffened and he slowly turned around, facing her. Another reason she shouldn't have come over was how she felt whenever he was close. He could touch her right here and she'd melt into his arms, giving him anything he asked.

"Oh, don't worry, little maiden. I plan on staying very sober where you're concerned." He glanced over her head, making a sound at the back of his throat. "After all, I'd hate to not be at my best, in case your new toy decides to take liberties."

"You mean like you did?" she shot back, glaring up at him, getting his full attention. "Maybe I'll let him do even more than you."

Drakon lowered his eyes to her, and then lowered his face so it was mere inches from her. "That would be a mistake."

"How so?"

"I think we both know that by now I'm the only one going to touch you."

"You don't own me, Drakon. I'm promised to another." She crossed her arms over her breasts, a mistake. His eyes went right to her chest and damn it to hell if her nipples didn't harder under the silk at that look. "You had your small chance to take what was offered and cast me aside **instead**." Quickly those eyes went back to her face. "Another gets what was offered."

"Don't play this game, Amelia."

"I'll play any game I wish." She turned and left him, but as much as she wanted to, she couldn't put on a smile for Kyril.

Before the meal was completely over, Amelia excused herself with the claim of having a major headache. She left, as quickly as she could, not even bothering to see if Drakon was still there or if he left with one of the maids.

Fifteen minutes later, she sat in her bathing pool, brooding over the words she had with Drakon. With no servants around, Amelia tended to herself. That was fine with her anyhow; she preferred to have the time alone. With her body slick and wet, Amelia walked up the steps and out of the pool. She grabbed the large drying cloth that she had draped over her bench, wrapping it around her slim body. It wasn't until she was covered that she felt eyes familiar on her.

Turning around slowly, she felt her heart pound in her chest the moment she spotted Drakon leaning against a marble stature of Anubis. He was bare from the waist up and Amelia saw every ripple on his chest. It was the first time that she saw him without a vest or shirt. Her hands itched to touch the soft patch of hair that ran from his stomach down to the hidden depths of his breeches. When her eyes traveled down his body, she was shocked to see that his boots were off and resting next to the stature also. In fact, it seemed that he had been waiting for her to finish her bath, and had removed some of his clothing in preparation to join her, she guessed, afterward.

Her sea green, defiant eyes, met his cool dark brown ones. His controlled look caused chills and a warning to flow within her. There was a reason he was here, within her room. However, she could not fathom what that reason might be.

The warning he gave her rang clearly in her head. He told her to *not* play a game with him, just as Alexis warned her of the burn. Well from the look on his face now, the way his eyes seemed to watch every move she made, Amelia figured that game was coming to an end and she was about to get burned.

"What are you doing here?" she demanded with a slight quiver to her voice. Her hands tightened on the knot that kept the cloth closed at her breasts, waiting to see what he was going to do or say. She hoped that the front she was putting up was good enough. Inside she was suddenly scared of what was to come.

Drakon raised one of his eyebrows, as he looked her over with a feverish expression. Both of his thumbs were hooked in the front of his breeches, as he looked her up and down.

"We have unfinished business, you and I," he answered her in a rough, thick voice.

Amelia took one step back. Caution slammed into her from the way he was looking at her. "There is nothing unfinished between us. I said what was needed to be said." She gave him a stern look that didn't reach her eyes. "Now leave!"

Drakon pushed off the statue and took a step closer. "No."

The way he told her no sent fear into her. Amelia was always used to her orders being met and followed, so when Drakon told her no she didn't know what to say. The only thing she could do was take another step back as he came forward.

"I don't know what kind of game you are playing... " She tried to put authority into her voice as she spoke to him, but her taking another step back didn't help her cause. "But I'm not playing and you won't get away with being in my chamber this time. I will tell Corydon."

Drakon took hold of the lacing in the front of his breeches. Keeping eye contract he tugged on the knot. "Wont I?" he challenged. "And telling him will only hurt that reputation you work so hard at keeping."

Amelia swallowed hard and worked even harder to not look down at his working hands. She was starting to shake as she took yet another step back, wary yet thrilled by his intentions.

Her foot touched the first step of the cooling bath water, and yet he still came at her.

Her mouth went dry the moment she saw all the laces pulled and Drakon bending over as the breeches slid down his hips and legs. Wide-eyed and breath sucking in sharply, she watched him straighten up, offering Amelia her first look at a man's body. The patch of hair that she found so fascinating went all the way down between his legs to a cock that stood hard and proud. She had heard some of the servants talk about a man's cock before, so her guess was that Drakon was sporting at least eight if not nine inches. Even the base of it was shocking. It was so thick that she knew one hand would not reach all the way around.

His waist narrow, hips firm and legs strong, as she looked him up and down. Her mouth opened in shock when he took his own hand and wrapped it around the base, stroking it gently. Nothing came to mind when she thought of something to say to him in order to get him to leave her room before things got way out of hand.

Water reached her knees before Amelia realized that Drakon backed her up in her own bath. She looked at him in a combination of helplessness and fascination at what he was going to do.

* * * *

Drakon followed her into the pool with his hands now at his sides. The cool water did nothing to his heated flesh or to the heavy hardness of his cock as he came toward her. His only thoughts were to rip that cloth and feel her skin touching his own.

Need slammed into him hard while he thought about her body hidden by the cloth. He stood as still as a statue watching her bath, watching and fighting with himself to not strip and join her. As he watched her, he thought about what it would be like to follow every one of those drops of water down her back with his tongue. To taste each inch of her flesh and feast upon it as if it was his last meal.

Ever since that last kiss, he couldn't seem to get her out of his mind. At night, Drakon thought his cock could not get harder, yet it had and that surprised him.

He worked hard at controlling the urge to take her from the water and place her naked beneath him. In all his years, not one woman ever caused his body to feel this alive. Not one turned him into a man who wanted nothing more than to conquer one woman as Drakon wanted to do right now. Since his return, he'd played the cat chasing the mouse, and now the cat was going to get *his* mouse and eat it.

"We... I mean... you can't be here," she tried again, her voice shaking when she spoke.

Drakon backed her up all the way to the other side. He stopped in front of her, looking down as she looked up at him. He wrapped one hand around her throat and rubbed his thumb over a throbbing vein.

"Drakon..." she started to say, but his thumb pressed on her lips, quieting her.

"Shhh." He rubbed her lips with his thumb, feeling the shake that went through her body. "Don't speak." He kept his voice low. "Don't command."

He moved her hands to her sides and touched the knot in the cloth. With a quick and somewhat rough jerk, he easily ripped **the cloth** from her body. She gasped, covering her breasts with both of her hands. Amelia breathed in harshly as he bent over, brushing his lips gently over hers.

"Do you remember our last kiss?" he asked her softly with his mouth mere inches from hers. "Because I have never forgotten it." He took the final step that was needed to press his body to hers. "It haunts my dreams.

Amelia opened her mouth as if to speak, but instead her hands touched his waist and moved up to his chest. Drakon flattened his hand at her throat again and slid down her chest, cupping one breast. He tested the weight, rubbing the nipple with his thumb.

Her hands went up to his neck and fingers raked into his hair, forcing his head down to her waiting mouth. She kissed him first, starting the game that would ignite the flame within both of them.

He moaned and brought one of her legs up to his waist, then the other, picking her up. He bent her backwards on the side of the pool, mouth-leaving mouth only to trail down her neck and shoulder. She moaned and tried to move closer to him.

Drakon licked his way down to her waiting breasts, sucking one hard nipple into the heated depths of his mouth. His hands skimmed down to her hot core finding her surprisingly wet and very much ready for him. This pleased him.

She dug her nails fiercely into his head as he went to work on her other nipple. Using two fingers, he pushed into her heated core. Drakon moaned against her breast as he thought about how good she was going to feel when he entered her. How blissful their coming together would be.

While he kissed her neck, shoulders, and mouth, his hands roamed over her legs, breasts and through her hair. Drakon was on fire and wanted to be inside her so badly he could barely withstand it.

He positioned the head of his cock at her gateway to heaven as he sat her on the edge of the pool. The kiss he gave her stole not only her breath but he hoped all of her senses as he rubbed the head of his penis against the wet heat.

He moved his mouth all over her body and hands up and down her legs as he gently nudged his hips forward. He licked a spot on her neck, tasting the mixture of the bathwater and salt of her sweat. Again, he pushed more of the aching hardness into her, stretching her innocence as his mouth moved over her neck and shoulder.

By all the gods, he thought, this was the one woman he had been waiting for his whole life. This was the one woman that could bring his raging soul peace at last!

Drakon moved his lips to her, kissing her deeply and plunging his tongue in her mouth, tasting the wine she drank at supper. He moaned into her mouth and moved further inside her, moaning at the gratification he felt when her body tightened around him. He relished in the thought that she was finally his!

He only stopped his hips once, and that was to bring her legs up to her chest and hold them there for her. She was open for him, sitting on the side of the pool. Open and in need, just as Drakon was.

He deepened the kiss even more as his hips jerked forward hard. He tore through her virginity and took her cry of pain in a kiss, just as he took the weeks of painful teasing.

He held his body still, not moving as he waited for the pain to subside in her, kissing her until he felt her body relax. After what seemed like long, excruciating minutes, when in fact it was mere moments, Drakon felt her body relax again. His mouth left hers to trail down her throat and shoulder, stopping to watch as he pulled out of her body only to slide back in. The thrill of watching their bodies as they came together seemed to give him extra pleasure.

"So beautiful," he said to her so softly.

* * * *

Amelia's head went back and her mouth opened in a silent cry of intense pleasure. The one thing that came to her mind as he moved within her was that this was the reason love play between a man and a woman was a well-hushed secret. The feelings that were racing within her were unlike anything she could or ever would be able to put into words.

She wrapped her legs tightly around his hips and her hands clutched onto the side of the pool. She closed her eyes in bliss while his hands roamed over her body, cupping her breasts and tweaking her nipples. Tighter and tighter, she felt her body being wound. Thinking to herself, Amelia wondered how much long this could go one. How much tighter could she be wounded? What she didn't know was that all answers would come in due time.

Drakon had his mouth everywhere as he thrust his hips in a steady, hard rhythm. There was not one inch of her body that he didn't taste or touch. He even left a few love bites around her breasts that she was starting to fall in love with.

A whimper escaped her lips. Her body was so close, felt so tightly wound, she didn't know what to do. Drakon wrapped an arm around her body, bringing her closer as he moved even faster. Chills raced down her spine and he hiked one leg higher on his hip. Her arms tightened around his neck and his cheek pressed against hers as the ride suddenly ended.

Amelia cried out as pleasure washed over her. She pressed her body as close to his as she could get, crying while he continued to move his hips in short, fast thrusts.

His sudden moan ricocheted in her ears as one arm went around her waist and the other up to the back of her neck, holding her tightly as he contracted inside her, causing the pleasure to last.

For the longest time both could only stay as they were, holding on to each other and breathing hard. Both were afraid to move, and neither really wanted to.

Hours later, Amelia woke from a dream suddenly. She sat straight up in her bed with the thin sheet covering her breasts and only half of her body. Hair fell into her face as she tried to get her breathing under control. She closed her eyes, telling herself that it was all a dream, nothing more. However, the dream she had was not just a dream. A slight lingering soreness between her legs told her that something major happened. Looking to her right it all came back to her.

In her bed, sleeping on his stomach with the sheet barely covering his rear, Drakon slept deeply. Both of them were naked, and in the middle of her room, close to her statue was his pile of clothes that he'd stripped from his body earlier. Amelia swallowed hard as her body continued to remind her that this was not a dream.

Running her hand into her hair, then over her face, she looked at the sleeping form of Drakon. "What have I done?" she asked herself in shock, "My God! What have I done?"

Chapter Four

Amelia sat alone at the table, waiting for the rest of the family to come for the morning meal, pushing her food around her plate not touching a damn thing. After waking up and seeing Drakon in her bed, realizing that it wasn't a dream, she quickly dressed and left.

She groaned at the mistake of leaving him there. If one of the servants came in and saw him—well she couldn't think about that. What she had to think about was what she would do now. She gave herself to Drakon and was expected to marry Kyril. How much more messed up could things get for her?

She couldn't sit here. The need to get away overwhelmed her. Amelia got up and left, not knowing where she was going. She just knew that if she saw her brother then she might blurt out what happened, just to get out of this marriage. Yet, if she did that, then there would be trouble for her and Drakon and she couldn't do that to him no matter what happened between them.

She rounded a corner and someone took hold of her arm, yanked her into one of the storage rooms. She heard the door close and then she was pushed up against the door. Amelia blinked and looked up at Drakon, his body so close she could feel his body heat.

"What are you doing?" she breathed out, fisting her hands in her dress so she wouldn't touch him. "Are you trying to get caught?"

The corner of his lips curled up and his eyes sparkled. "You slipped out of the bed without a word." He reached down, touched her lips with his fingers. The contact had her struggling to breathe. "Lucky for you I was already dressed when your servants came in." Amelia's eyes widened. "I told them I was looking for you."

"It shouldn't have happened," she whispered. "I'm the maiden of the house engaged to another."

Drakon shook his head. "You use to be." He ran one finger from her lips down her chin to her throat were he closed his hand. "Now you belong to me. Kyril will never have you."

She swallowed hard, got control over herself, and wrapped one of her own hands around his wrist. "No." She jerked it away, ducked under his arm, and moved away.

"No?"

"That's right." Amelia turned, facing him. She raised her chin. "I'm not yours and as far as I'm concerned last night never happened. It was only a dream."

He rushed her, forcing Amelia to take several steps back until she touched the wall. She raised her hands up as if to ward him off.

Drakon slapped her hands away, grabbed both of her wrists, and jerked her to him. "Shall I show you how real your dream is?" One arm went around her waist, holding her close and tight. He picked her up and pressed her back to the wall and yanked up her skirt.

"Don't," she whimpered, feeling her body waking to his touch.

His hand touched her bare rear and Amelia moaned. She closed her eyes, rested her face against his as he kissed her neck, and worked their clothing the way he wanted. One single tear slipped from her eye as she felt him enter her body. She stretched for him, throbbed in need, and took everything he had.

He moved inside her, stroked the inner flesh, drawing her mad with the slowness. Amelia fisted her hand into his hair and pulled, bringing forth a hiss from him. Drakon stopped kissing at her shoulder and throat and moved up to stare at her. He kept moving, kept filling her with his flesh and she moved with him. Mouth open, Amelia thrust back against him when he entered her, matching him stroke for stroke.

Drakon kissed her deeply, his tongue plunging into her mouth. When she wrapped her legs and arms around him, he picked up his pace. He took her hard, pushing her back up against the wall with each inward motion. The release she felt hit her fast. Amelia cried out in his mouth, digging her nails into his shoulders. She shook with her pleasure as he kept moving inside her. She felt him swell, could even feel the contractions that came with his own moan.

"I'll find a way," Drakon panted against her shoulder. His body was still locked with her and she held onto him tightly. "I can't lose you now. I'll find a way to get you out of this. I promise."

"Please don't promise something you can't deliver," she sighed, resting her head on his shoulder. "Corydon won't let me out of this and Kyril has wanted me for years. He's not going to let me go."

"I never make a promise I don't intend on delivering. You're mine Amelia and no one else is going to take you from me."

They snuck from the room and she went back to her chamber. She took a long bath, and then dressed in her warm white leggings and long white fur trimmed top with silver belt at the waist and the silver crown for a morning ride. As she was getting her feet into her boots she got a message that Corydon wanted to see her in the great hall.

Amelia's hands began to shake. She feared that her brother discovered what she had done with Drakon. Shaking it off she finished and left her room, her stomach turning with each step she took.

The double doors were open. Corydon stood at the end in front of the throne. To her left, Alexis stood talking with one his men that came with him. To his right, Drakon stood, arms crossed over his chest, legs spread. He didn't look at all happy, and he didn't look at her either when she entered.

"I was starting to wonder if you were ill," Corydon said.

"Just getting ready for a morning ride," she said, unable to stop herself from glancing in Drakon's direction. She saw the quick smirk on his face before he turned his head and covered his mouth with his hand.

"Well, that's perfect then." Corydon clapped his hands together, smiling. "Kyril will join you."

It was only with him mentioning Kyril's name that she noticed him not there. Taking a deep breath and preparing herself for the rage that was to come she said, "And why would I want to do that?"

Corydon gave her a very strange smile, scratched the side of his head, and laughed in a weird way. "It was a long time ago, Amelia. You need to let it go."

"Not to me it wasn't. How the hell can you say that to me? You weren't there!"

"I'm telling you to stop this!" Corydon yelled, rushed up to her and grabbing both of her arms hard. "You will respect my wishes in my house just like you will accept that this marriage is going to happen." He narrowed his eyes on her, gave her a shake. "He's to be your husband."

She lost her temper and cool. Amelia twisted out of his hold and slapped him as hard as she could, ignoring the stinging to her hand. "I would rather die by his blade then let that murdering bastard touch me. How could you forget that he raped and killed our mother? You were there! Does the scar on your face not remind you?" She backed away so he couldn't take hold of her again. "I don't understand you, Corydon. What has he done to make you just hand me over like this?"

"We need—"

"No!" she cut him off, shaking her head. "No, it's what you need or something they've done. I never thought in all my years you would just hand me off to him like this. But then again, I guess I never really did know you after all." She turned and left before more could be said. Before other things, that one couldn't take back slipped out.

* * * *

Drakon didn't move a muscle when Amelia left. Inside, he fumed, raging, in fact, over the way Corydon was handling things.

"Marrying her to him won't stop his blood lust," Drakon said to Corydon. "It'll only ease it for a time. He and his father will still want to strip this land clean for themselves."

"Stay out of this, Drakon," Alexis said.

"No, I'm not!" Drakon snapped. He moved from where he stood, going over to Corydon. "If you need another hand in this war then I'll be it. I'll marry her and give you what you need."

"You," Corydon snorted. "What do you have to offer by a name? The Drystals destroyed everything."

"I can give you Kyril's' head," Drakon stated through his teeth.

Corydon shook his head, "The deal's done. I won't go back on my word and I trust Kyril won't either."

"Then you're more of a damn fool then I ever thought you'd be." Drakon glanced at Alexis before turning on his heels and leaving the room. He walked in long strides back to his chamber. Each step that pounded on the tile floor matched the pounding rage he felt inside.

Drakon went into his room with a kick to the doors. They opened and banged against the walls, and with just as much force, he closed them with a deafening slam. Dropping his sword to the bed, he picked up the glass on the table with the intentions of having a drink. Instead, he threw it as hard as he could.

"Were you going to tell me?" Alexis stood in the doorway, holding the double doors open. Drakon glared at him. "No I didn't think so."

"What do you want, Alexis?" Drakon asked slowly. He wasn't in the mood to talk with anyone, least of all him.

Alexis walked into his room, closing the doors. "You know, when we left here and returned to Rome, I knew then there was something between you and her, but I couldn't put my finger on it. I watched the change in you over the years. Saw how you cleaned up, in a way. Didn't go out whoring like you use to, but it never did dawn on me that it was all because of her." He went to the fire, knelt down, and started to rebuild it. "Corydon won't let you have her. In his eyes, there is already a treaty between him and Drystal. He won't break that for nothing."

"Oh I'm sure there is something to break this fucking contract up," Drakon growled. Alexis glanced over his shoulder at Drakon. "Kyril isn't going to touch her." Drakon said this time through his teeth this time, barely controlling the boiling rage inside. "His fucking father showed him how to rape and kill. The bastard killed her mother in front of her eyes and Corydon wants her to marry and lie with him!" he yelled. "Hell no!"

"Drakon—"

"If he tries to marry her off he'll not only lose her because I *will* take her away, but I'll be at war with him," he said with venom. "You mark my words." He pointed his finger at Alexis to emphasize his point.

Alexis stood up, turned, and crossed his arms over his chest. "You would rage war over her?"

Drakon knew what Alexis was asking. To voice it to a second and in his case Alexis was his second that he would go to war for a woman was a strong commitment. Just about as strong as if he was signing a treaty with marriage on the table and once it was voiced and known how one or the other felt, you couldn't go back on it. It was a pack that the Romans took very seriously.

"Yes," Drakon stated. "I would."

"Do you love her?"

Drakon met Alexis' eyes. The question of love happened to come up one other time with him, and he pondered the thought. Now, as he stood staring at his best friend, a brother to him, Drakon didn't hesitate in giving the answer. "Yes. I love her and am willing to die for her."

Alexis took a deep breath and let it out in a rush, then rubbed his face to the back of his neck. "Damn it, Drakon."

"You told me just the other day how unhappy you and Ismame are." Alexis opened his mouth, but Drakon went on quickly. "I refuse to be unhappy any longer. I love her, Alexis, and I don't give a fuck anymore that I hurt. She's mine and I'm going to have her."

Again, Alexis took a deep breath. "Kyril isn't going to let her go either. If the man has put war aside just to marry her for Christ sakes, then you know he wants her real bad."

"Tough shit."

"It's not that simple, Drakon. A contract has been made and signed. Corydon and Kyril aren't going to break it."

"Then I guess something else is going to have to."

"What the hell are you talking about?" Drakon didn't answer him, just grabbed another cup, and poured himself a drink. "No! Tell me that you didn't." He didn't look at Alexis. Keeping his head down he took a big drink. "Son of a bitch! How could you do that?"

"It happened."

"Happened my ass! It never just happens, not with you!" Alexis yelled.

Drakon's shoulders slumped and he rubbed the back of his neck.

"Do you even realize what you've done? What Corydon or that bastard is going to do to her *once* they find out?" Alexis said.

Drakon opened his mouth and this time Alexis cut him off. "And they will find out, Drakon. Kyril isn't stupid. He's going to pick up that something is going on between the two of you, if he just watches you two. Motherfucker!"

"Kyril has wanted this planet and everything they've got since he first set foot on it when he was sixteen," Drakon said through his teeth. "What the hell happened to make them withdraw and kept them at bay I don't know. What I do know is that even if, by some small fate of the gods, Kyril marries Amelia, he won't be satisfied until he has all of Egypt for himself. Do you know that he has tried at least twice since I've tried to rebuild Corinth to conqueror it again? Made damn sure no one will come back. Half of my people are the people that that damn family has scattered all over the universe. It's taken me three years to build my home up and he has come right behind me to tear it back down. I'm not going to let that cruel bastard have her or anyone else."

Alexis rubbed the back of his neck. "You may have started war already without them even knowing it."

"If you're expecting me to feel guilt over this, you're wasting your time."

"Oh I know that. I've yet to see you have guilt or anything." Alexis headed for the doors.

"Where're you going?"

"Well, since you've started a fight I think I'm going to send my son home for safety. I don't wish to put him in danger and I'm sure as shit, once Kyril or Corydon discovers that the maiden of the house is no longer a maiden, they're going to want to kill something. Better to get him out of the line of fire, don't you think?"

"And Ismame?"

Alexis sighed again, "Well, let's face it. I think that relationship is over so if she wants to stay here who am I to stop her?"

"And the treaty?"

"I have a son. As long as he lives that treaty **and** peace will remain."

* * * *

Amelia didn't go riding as she planned but returned to her room where she sat in front of her vanity, staring at nothing. Her mind wouldn't stop reliving what Corydon said to her in the hall and how much he seemed to change overnight.

"And the proud maiden sits alone, brooding over what she can't control."

Amelia raised her head. Behind her stood Ismame dressed in a loose flowing blue gown that hung from her shoulder. Around her waist a gold belt to match the cold crown on her head.

"Your demons have come home." Ismame strolled into her room acting like a goddess. "To claim what he has always wanted." She stopped behind Amelia and reached out to touch her hair. "You."

Amelia moved before she was touched, distancing herself from her sister.

"You always did think you were better than me," Ismame snapped. "Little miss perfect. Always had to have things her way. Well guess what, little sister?" She extended her arms out, and laughed. "Not this time. This time you must suck it up and do what is expected of you, just like me."

"Is that what you think of your marriage?" she asked. Amelia worked to keep her voice level. There was something about Ismame's eyes. Something that she couldn't put her finger on. "A duty? I would have thought that being with a man like Alexis was more than satisfactory. He appears like he would treat you as a goddess."

Ismame snorted, "You would think that. Then, you are young and still innocent. Now take a man like Kyril," she sighed, looking like she was dreaming. "There is a real man."

Amelia frowned, "Ismame what's wrong with you? How can you stand there acting all dreamy over a man that killed our mother?"

Ismame shrugged, "Things happen in war."

"Are you out of your mind?" Amelia gasped. "I saw him rape mother and you stand there like you want to be his lover. It's disgusting!"

Ismame moved fast. So fast that Amelia didn't get the chance to move away from her. Her sister grabbed her wrist tight, but Amelia didn't make a sound. "Kyril has power and its best you learn that now. Power is everything. If you don't have it, you are nothing. Kyril has plenty of it, and I bet he'll share it with me. For a sweet price."

"You're crazy. Kyril is nothing more than a brutal man who will ruin us all if given a chance."

Ismame struck fast. She slapped Amelia so hard on the side of the face that Amelia took two side steps. "I'm going to take everything that should've been mine. Once Kyril sates his lust over you, I'll be there."

"You're wrong."

Ismame raised her hand up again to hit Amelia.

"Am I interrupting?"

They both turned towards the door. Kyril stood in the doorway, holding the thick double doors open wide. He pushed away, strolled into the room as if he owned it. Ismame lowered her hand, bowed to him and quickly brushed past him out of the room, closing the doors behind her.

Amelia rubbed her cheek, staring at him, trying to keep distance between them without letting him know it. One eyebrow went up, indicating that he did notice.

"You know, ever since I got here I've felt as if something has been preventing us from having any time together," he said.

"Maybe that should be a sign then."

He smiled, walked around her room, looking at her things, touching. "I've come to ask you to join me for lunch. Thought it might be the best chance we can get to talk."

"If I refuse?"

"I hope you won't. I'd hate to have to play the brother card, if you know what I mean." He bowed. "In an hour then."

He left, and she was about to go for her ride again, but once more her brother had other things to say about it. He sent a dress and a short message to not be late. An hour later she entered the guest chamber where Kyril was preparing for a meal.

"Just in time," Kyril said. "Please, come in."

Amelia swallowed hard. She jumped when he closed the doors behind her, and cringed slightly at his touch on her back, guiding her to the table.

Taking her seat, hands in her lap, eyes on his every move, she waited. Kyril stood next to her, picked up a bottle, and twisted the top. It popped, and she jumped again.

"Very jumpy, I see," he stated.

"I'm not sure how to be alone with a man," She told him softly. *Lord I hope he believes this act!*

He poured some wine into her glass before taking his seat and pouring himself some. "I should hope not." He put the bottle back into its ice bath. Amelia looked everywhere but at him. "You are the loveliest woman I've ever seen." When she finally did look at him, Kyril took a drink. "And you don't trust me." She raised one eyebrow up. He smiled. "I see it in your eyes."

"Should I?"

He put his glass down and leaned right, resting his arm on the table. He had one ring on his finger, his middle finger, a ruby in the shape of a D, which he played with. "Men of great strength always have a past they are not proud of. I'm not proud of mine."

"But I get that strange feeling that you are. Your past is what's made you the man you are now."

"And what kind of man is that?"

Amelia saw the humor in his eyes. He was trying to play with her or tease her. She wasn't sure which. "The kind that is used to getting what he wants."

He had a bemused grin on his lips, one that she wanted desperately to slap away. "That I am." He picked his glass back up, taking another drink. He made this slapping sound, as if he was trying to get an extra taste. "This is very good. You should try some."

"What do you really want?" she asked, leaning forward.

That was a slight mistake. Kyril took hold of her hand before she could move away. He brought it up to his face, holding onto her wrist also with his other hand. He bent the hand to expose the wrist before lowering his lips to it. His cold eyes locked with hers, sending fresh chills down her spine.

"You," He stated his deep voice vibrating as he spoke. She wasn't stupid, and after being with Drakon she knew what that sound meant.

"And if I refuse?"

She felt his tongue touch her wrists before his lips pressed a kiss. "I have something for you." Kyril let her arm go and stood up. She shook, watching him head over to the bed where two boxes rested. The smaller one he picked up and brought over to the table. Her plate of food was moved aside and the box put in its place. He then moved behind her, resting both hands on her bare shoulders. "I've had this for a long time. Been waiting for the day I could give it to you."

Kyril leaned over her and opened the lid. Inside was a large gold and ruby necklace. The rubies were big, the largest in the middle as big as the palm of her hand and the others about as big as a knuckle. He picked it up, turned it, and placed it around her neck. It was very heavy.

He moved to her left, still kneeling down. She swallowed hard when he touched it, his finger trailing along then down to touch her chest and the top curves of her breasts briefly. She couldn't control her breathing, and was pretty sure he was taking it as a sign that his touch was exciting her.

When he stood up, his hand moved up to her throat, cupped under her chin and the other at the back of her head. Together he moved her head back and she closed her eyes. Amelia couldn't look at him.

Kyril kissed her.

It wasn't a peck of a kiss, or anything simple. No, this kiss was deep and slightly forceful. He was bold with his kiss by working his tongue against her closed mouth until she was powerless by his hold to stop him. He touched the inside of her mouth, moaning against her, holding her so she couldn't break away. When he finally backed off and became gentle, Amelia somehow ended it.

"You take a liberty that isn't yours to take," she said softly.

He was still close. Close enough that she could feel his breath upon her skin, smell the wine he just drank.

"Refuse me, Amelia, and I'll burn your home to the ground." He kissed her again, brushing his lips against her own. "And turn the offer of wife into my personal whore instead."

Amelia pushed him away and twisted out from the chair. She rushed to the doors, only to be stopped by his hand slamming over her head and body pressed up against her. He took hold of her arm, turning her roughly to face him.

She was breathing hard and fast, in both her fear and adrenalin. "At least I understand fully and see your true colors," she breathed out.

He grabbed her throat, holding her tightly. "I have lusted for you since the moment I laid eyes on you. No other in my bed has been able to sate my desire for you. Either by the honor of marriage or as a whore, I will have you."

"Never!" she gasped out, holding onto his arm. "I'll never be yours. Never lay with the man who killed my mother."

His hold loosened and she slapped his hand away, taking a deep breath. "So you do remember."

"How could I ever forget?" A single tear slipped free, trailing down her cheek. "I see what you did to her in my nightmares. I'll never forget."

"I'm sorry about that. I didn't know she was your mother and my father was putting a large amount of pleasure on me to have my first kill and conquering."

"And how little that comforts me."

"I didn't ask you here to upset you."

"Then why did you ask me here? I mean, I'm a bit confused since I'm sure you know just as my brother does that I don't want this marriage."

"You don't believe in second chances?"

"I believe that there are some people in this world who should never have second chances."

"Does that pertain to me?"

"Yes, now let me go." She turned at the door to leave again, only to have him grab hold of her wrist, jerking her to his chest where he wrapped both arms tightly around her. "Let go!"

"I've waited a very long time for you," he said low, his eyes darkening. Being so close to him, Amelia felt his hard cock pressed against her. He also shocked her by pressing her up against the door. "Thought about nothing else but you." Panic began to set in when he shifted and held her with one arm, the other going down her side and back up her leg, picking it up and placing it on his hip. "I look forward to the night when you will be mine finally."

"Then you will be sorely disappointed," she hissed in his face, pushing against his chest. "I'm never going to be yours."

The hand that had been holding her leg up moved back to her face.

With knuckles, he touched her check; the same spot where Ismame slapped her. Amelia turned her face away but it didn't stop him from touching her.

"You are so very beautiful," he whispered, leaning closer. She held her breath; waiting for the assault, she just knew would come. No, Kyril brushed his lips over her cheek tenderly. "So very soft." He leaned in to kiss her again, and she turned her head. Therefore, his lips touched her cheek, back to her ear, down the throat and back up to the ear. "I mean what I say, maiden of the house. I will have you, one way, or the other," he whispered. "That choice is yours." He pushed away from her and cleared his throat. "I request that you wear my gift always in good faith to our engagement. In the morning I'll have your gown sent to you."

"Gown?" she frowned.

"It is our tradition, the Drystal people to gift the bride with a special wedding gown, along with a necklace. I'm requesting our marriage to take place in three days." He bowed to her. "Good evening, my Lady."

Dinner that night ended up being very formal and small. Ismame snapped out of her emotional state and dressed in a soft blue dress with gold. Alexis had a silk top to match her dress and sat next to her. Across from him, Drakon with Amelia and Kyril at the far end of the table with Croydon right across taking the head.

She dressed in a black leather corset with sparkling crystals in the long flowing skirt. Matching leather gloves with fingers rose up her arms to the point where the corset met; making it look like it was off her shoulders. Her hair she had pulled up off her shoulders, wrapped in leather thongs, and around her neck a choker that had chains going down the whole front of the outfit to the bottom of the skirt. She didn't put the necklace on or wear the gown, something that Kyril did notice by the glare that he cast her way when she entered.

Corydon ordered a large meal and toasted Kyril. Soup, fish, three different kinds of meat and dessert, plus the wine flowed almost too freely. When they were eating the dessert, Corydon stood up with his wine glass in hand. Amelia almost feared what might come out of his mouth next.

"It has been requested, by your bridegroom to have the wedding date moved to an earlier time," Corydon said. Amelia looked down the table at Kyril who happened to be smiling. Those damn cold eyes of his landed on her and he winked. "I've granted the request."

Amelia gasped, giving her full attention back to Corydon. "You can't!"

"I can, and I have."

"Congratulation," Ismame said, her glass rose up.

Amelia ignored her. "Corydon, please."

"Two days from now you will marry Kyril Drystal, the treaty complete and this fighting over with for good."

Amelia didn't bother with containing her anger. She pushed away from the table, facing her brother. "You force me to do this and you will no longer be my brother."

"It is done, Amelia," Corydon said. "So fighting it is pointless."

She turned from her seat, heading down the table, stopping next to Kyril. "You won't get what you're after, I promise you that."

She left the room, head high, hands shaking. With as much dignity as she had left, Amelia went back to her room, the tears falling. One thought, however, hit her as she walked down the hall. What would they both think once it was discovered she was no longer the maiden of the house? What would her brother and Kyril do then when they learned she gave her innocence away to another?

Chapter Five

Ismame strolled around Kyril's chamber, waiting for him to come out of the bathing room. It had been years since she last stepped foot in this room and nothing had changed. She wrinkled her nose when she looked at the bed, recalling how her new husband took her there many times in the night, making her so sore she thought she wouldn't be able to walk.

"Have you ever asked yourself why you desire her?" she asked Kyril the moment he came out of the bath, a drying cloth in his hand up at his chest. He was naked, dripping wet and a sight that had her tingling to touch. "And what might happen once you slake your lust?" He cocked his head, the cloth dropping with his arm. "Or even question if she is still pure."

"You doubt your sister?" Kyril asked.

"I doubt many things." She strolled up to him, touched his chest with one finger, and moved it down the middle.

"Such as?"

Flattening her hand on his chest and moving it down she wrapping it around his cock, which she desperately wanted to taste. She stroked him and he hardened to her touch. "I doubt the strength of my brother," she spoke low and soft. "I doubt that my sweet sister is sweet, and I doubt that you want the peace you claim you want."

Kyril's breathing picked up with her hand movements, but he didn't stop her. "You don't think I want peace?" he panted softly.

"Oh I think you want many things, only peace isn't one of them."

He smiled and took a step back, stopping her strokes. Ismame stayed put while he dried his hair more, tossed the cloth aside, and went over to the table where he poured himself a drink. Not once did he cover his nakedness.

"You're right about one thing. I do want your sister." Filling up a cup, Kyril picked it up and took a drink. "Wanted her from the first moment I saw those big eyes of hers watching me."

"Did you enjoy the killing?" Ismame strolled up behind him, wrapped her arms around his waist, hands going right back to his cock. "The raping?"

Kyril laughed softly. "Oh, you like to play dangerously, don't you?"

"I like men who know how to take what they want."

"And are you the kind of woman who gets what she wants?"

"I am."

"Then show me what it is you want."

Ismame licked her lips and went down to her knees before him. She opened her mouth and sucked his cock in, moaning at the pleasure. Kyril's mouth went open, his head down and eyes locked on her. She sucked him, bobbed her head back and forth and he matched her with his hips. He thrust his cock in and out, making her take more of the long member. She took it all, sliding it down her throat loving how thick he was, how long.

Ismame moaned again right before she popped it out of her mouth and stood up. She reached for her shoulders and pushed the grown off, letting it all fall to her feet.

He looked her naked body over. "And your husband? What will he think, knowing that you are trying to seduce your way into my good graces?"

"Is that what I'm doing?"

He moved fast, grabbing her by the back of her head, fisting his hand in her hair. "Don't play games with me. You'll lose."

She reached behind her head, pried his fingers from the locks. "I can assure you, my Lord, I'm playing no games. You want my sister and I'm more than willing for you to have her."

"Then what is it you want."

Ismame licked his chest, followed it up by a kiss. "I want the throne of Egypt. You put me there and all my riches will be yours, as well as myself."

Again Kyril laughed. "Who says I can't have it all *without* giving you the crown?"

"You need me, and I'm about to show you just how much." Once more she went down to her knees, taking hold of his cock. She kissed the top, flicking it with her tongue.

"And what about your husband?" he breathed out.

She pulled back, licking the underside before speaking. "Kill him. I don't care." She took it back into her mouth, pulling on it harder, sucking it faster.

* * * *

Amelia stood in front of her window, stared out at the Nile, wind blowing softly against her cool flesh. She finished her bath, slipped into her robe and just stood there thinking about what she was going to do. She had to come up with something to get out of this upcoming marriage, but could only come up with one thing. Telling Kyril that she was no longer a virgin. Her gut told her that would be enough for him to break off this deal and go home.

Now granted, Corydon would fly off once it was known, but she would at least be free from Kyril, at least she hoped.

Below she saw a carriage pull up and Alexis come out with the baby in his arms, Luna right behind him. She watched him help Luna inside then hand the baby off to her, close it, and tap the sides. It pulled away, leaving Alexis standing alone.

"I told him to take the baby away from here."

Amelia jumped and turned, her hand to her throat. "Drakon! What—what are you doing here?" He stood in front of the closed doors and slid the bolt in place, locking them in. "You shouldn't be here. We can't do this again."

"Says who?" He walked towards her slowly, unbuttoning his shirt, opening it and letting it fall to the floor behind him.

Her mouth went dry. Bare skin came into view causing her hands to itch just to touch it, to kiss and feel his skin against hers. The moment his hands went to his pants, she closed her eyes and turned her back on him.

"Please don't do this to me again," she whispered.

She felt the heat of his body next to her before he said a word. Knew he stood right behind her and felt powerless to fight him.

"I've been driving myself nuts wondering if he tried to touch you at lunch," Drakon said in her ear. "Did he?"

She couldn't open her eyes when his body pressed against hers. She could feel through her robe his nakedness, his hardness pressing against her backside. She pressed back against him, opened her eyes, and turned her head to his left arm as it slid around her shoulders. Amelia opened her mouth and bit his arm and Drakon hissed in her ear.

"Yes," she sighed, rubbing herself against him. "He touched me."

"Is that all?"

She licked the spot that she bit, shaking her head. "No. He kissed me also."

Drakon growled in her ear right before his right arm came down and he jerked open her robe, exposing her breasts to the cool air. She moaned when his hand closed over one globe, squeezing the mound.

His other hand also moved and, with another yank, her robe slid to the floor, leaving her naked before him. Hot hands slid down her legs, around the knees, parting her where she stood. He cupped her mound, teasing the swollen clit with the tip of a finger, driving her instantly mad with desire and need. She wanted to turn around to face him, but Drakon kept her standing where she was, her back to him, facing the Nile River.

"You're wet, little maiden." His voice had a purity to it when he spoke in her ear. "Is that for me, or him?"

Amelia thought she was going to die from this teasing. She moved her hips, using his finger, trying to get him to touch her harder. His cock teased her rear also. The head went back and forth between the two cheeks, to the point of her almost begging him to be inside her.

"You!" she panted. "Only for you."

He turned her around, keeping his body pressed to hers. Together they walked to the bed, but he didn't put her on it. Instead, Drakon tuned her once more away from him, bent her over face first over the bed with her rear up in the air.

Her legs were parted and two fingers entered her from behind. She moaned, resting her head down on the covers, hands fisting into the sheets. In and out those fingers of his moved, driving her insane with need.

"You are very wet for me," he said, quickening his pace. "Just how I like you. Ready and in need for only me."

"Yes," she gasped, pushing back every time he withdrew from her. "Drakon please!"

"Anything for you, my maiden."

His fingers left her body and she would have whimpered from the loss but he replaced them with his whole length of flesh between his own legs. Amelia moaned into the blankets when in one fluid motion he was inside her, parting her. Drakon was so thick and so strong with his thrust that it not only brought her up to her toes, but it had her feeling the tightening of her own body again. She didn't feel the pain, only intense pleasure.

"Yeah, tighten up on me like that," he moaned behind her, his body slapping into her. "Milk me."

She tried to push back against him, but it was pointless. He was power behind her. Taking her like an animal who was reassuring himself that this was his woman and she loved it. She gasped, panted, and fought to get each breath she took. The pleasure was a mixture of agony and a gnawing need she never knew. She wanted it to end and keep going at the same time.

"Don't stop," she moaned, shaking her head, feeling the wave that was about to hit her.

She cried out in her bedding. The blankets and sheet muffling her. Behind her she could hear Drakon moan, but it also sounded like a faint cry. Her climax washed through with star blinding pleasure. She felt herself contract against him, could feel him shake behind her and the swelling inside. She couldn't explain the sound that came from Drakon. Amelia only knew that she wanted to hear it again.

He fell on top of her, taking them both down to the floor. His arms went around her body, holding her tight as he jerked inside her. Somehow, that gave her one more orgasm, and pushed her into a short crying spell.

It took some time before either could move, and when she got control of herself, Drakon turned over, sitting on the floor. He pulled Amelia to him, placing her between his legs with arms tightly around her. They sat like that, saying nothing, just holding each other.

"If I refuse him, he'll burn Egypt to the ground," she said after some time passed. "And turn me into his whore."

"Egypt is already doomed." Drakon sighed. "The day your brother thought this plan up he started destroying the people. A Drystal knows nothing about peace only destruction."

"I don't think I can do this," she whispered. "I don't want to be in the same room with him."

"I know," he sighed, resting his forehead on her shoulder. "I just need a little bit of time."

"For what?"

"For my men to show up."

Amelia turned in his arms, facing him. "Why?" She frowned not understanding.

"Because everything's going to turn very ugly soon. I won't let Kyril have you and the moment Corydon lets Kyril know that I've also made an offer he's going to react very nasty."

"You made an offer?" She turned in his arms, looking him in the eye.

"Yes, I made an offer. I don't want to lose you." He reached up, touching the side of her face.

"Why would you do that?"

"Because I love you."

She felt like melting in his arms right then. Amelia turned in his arms, pressed him back down on the floor and laid over him. "You love me?"

His arms went around her, hands flat on her backside. "With all my heart."

She smiled big. "I have to say I didn't think you were ever going to say those words to me."

"And I never thought I'd say them either."

She leaned down, kissing him, letting her feelings come out in the kiss. "I love you too," she whispered against his lips. "I have since that very first kiss you gave me, and I'll love you with my last breath." With a sigh, she rested her head on his shoulder, enjoying him holding her. After a few minutes went by, Amelia told him what Kyril said. "He's going to have Corydon move the wedding date up."

"To when?"

"Couple of days."

"That's too soon."

"What am I going to do?"

"Well, for now we're going to play this game that your brother and Kyril have started and to keep you safe you need to stop staring at me so much. You can't keep looking for me when he's around. Kyril isn't stupid. He'll figure out that something is going on." He sighed in her hair. "I shouldn't have been as stupid as to take you in the bath. Not being the maiden of the house has put you in a very dangerous position. Your innocence is what he hungers for the most and is willing to do anything to have."

"I'll be alright," she said. "No one knows about us."

"And as much as I hate to say this, we need to keep it that way for now. I hate how I've put you in danger just because of my need and desire to simply be with you won out over the logic in my brain."

"You had logic?" Her eyebrows rose and a mocking smile spread across her face. "I never knew."

"You know, I don't think I've had the pleasure yet of giving you a nice spanking."

"For what?"

"For all the damn teasing you've done to me. It isn't nice to tease a man like you have. It tends to make them walk into bedrooms and seduce them."

"Well then, I'll just have to make sure I do things right then." She sat up, straddling him, licking her lips at the feel of him getting hard under her. "I have heard talk that this position is very enjoyable. Is it true?"

"Why don't you see for yourself?"

"I think I will." She reached down between them, took hold of his cock, and posed it at her entrance. Keeping eye contact, Amelia lowered herself onto him, taking every sweet hard inch.

Instinct kicked in and Amelia went with the flow. She moved on him like she would riding her horse and by the gods she loved each and every sensation, every pleasurable feeling that hit her. Breaking their eye contact, she arched backwards, mouth open in bliss. Drakon's hands moved to her hips then up her belly to breasts that were so sensitive, nipples so hard, she shivered each time he touched them.

Her ride didn't last as long as what she would've liked. To soon the sensations of her climax approached and by the way, Drakon started to moan. She lost the battle and climaxed. He followed, sitting up, holding her close, lips sucking on one hard nipple. She lost control of her emotions then. Amelia held him tight against her breasts, the tears falling freely down her face. She didn't want the night to end, didn't want their time to end, but knew it had to soon. He would have to leave her arms, her bed, before the sun came up. Leave her to deal with Kyril and her brother.

"If only we could stay like this forever," she sighed.

"Soon."

"Then love me. Love me tonight as if it's our last night."

He stood up, and together they went over to the bath where he washed her then himself. Drakon led her back to the bed placing her in the middle, legs open just for him.

"You're everything I want," he told her. He could see the glistening of her pussy and his mouth watered to taste it. The few times they came together, it was quick. Drakon didn't get to love her, as he wanted to. Tonight, he was going to love every inch of her body. Tonight, he was going to make love to her as if she was his wife and one day he vowed to himself, she would be. "Hold that leg just like that." He told her as he moved to the bed, bending one leg up. "I like it like that."

Drakon closed his eyes and touched the inside of her bent leg with his lips. Inhaled, taking in the sweet smell of her arousal. He moved his mouth up and down a couple of times before stopping and putting a kiss on her wet mound. He felt Amelia shiver and kissed her again there before opening his mouth and touching the tip of his tongue between the folds. He tasted her for the first time, moaning at the pleasure and that pleasure pounded right between his legs.

Using his thumbs, he parted her and went in. He licked and sucked her from her rear all the way to her clit. She quickly began breathing hard and fast, her hands fisted into his hair, pressing him closer each time he touched her clit.

"Oh," she moaned when he closed his lips around the nub and sucked, pushing two fingers into her. "Drakon, its close."

He moved his fingers in and out of her and looked up. "Then let me see if I can push you over some." He closed his mouth back on her clit and sucked hard, increasing the pace of his fingers. He also teased her rear with another.

Amelia bucked under him; her breathing became a pant mixed with moaning. He felt her tighten up and right before she peaked, he pushed one finger into her ass. She screamed, pressing his face into her pussy and pulling at his hair.

Her orgasm was music to his ears. Drakon kept sucking, fucking, and pulling on her to draw out each ripple inside of her. When the hands that pulled at his hair loosened up, he finally stopped sucking but not moving his fingers inside her.

"Turn over." He moved up enough for her to flip over to her stomach. Still he moved his fingers inside her, and moved them back to tease her rear. "I love how you taste." He licked up her spine to her shoulder where he bit and kissed her, placing his body on top of hers. "I think I could feast upon you for hours."

He kept kissing and biting on her and Amelia reached back, once more pulling on his hair. "Please," she panted, grinding her pussy against his hand. "I want you inside me."

"Do you now?" He teased her rear again before pushing two fingers inside as far as they would go. She was tight back there, but so willing that she welcomed it by pushing back.

"Yes!" she hissed, bucking under him. "Please."

Drakon moved up to his knees, but kept his fingers inside her. "Then get up on your knees for me." She did and he moaned. "God what a beautiful sight." He kissed one cheek then the other before biting her. When he finally did remove his fingers she groaned, but moaned again after he slapped her ass. "Two hours isn't going to be nearly enough for me. I want you all night long, but we can't."

"Don't talk," she panted. "Don't waste our time by talking."

He parted the globes and leaned in, licking the small puckered ring of her rear. Down he moved to her pussy, enjoying the whimper that slipped past her lips.

"Do you want me here?" he asked and flicked his tongue against the swollen lips before moving back. "Or here?" With his tongue only he pushed against the ring, but it wouldn't give. "You have to tell me so I'll know which one to go to."

"That's not fair," she panted.

He chuckled at her as he went back and forth. "And why's that?"

Amelia ended up surprising him by standing up on her knees, grabbing his hair from behind and pulling him to the bed. He laughed as she placed him on his back and came over him.

"Because I might want them both." She smiled at him. "You have me on fire, Drakon. I burn worse than the other times."

Drakon was about to say something but all thought left him. She kissed his chest, sucked on a nipple the same way he was sucking on her. Lower she went and it took all of his concentration to keep breathing. He had a thought that she might take him into her mouth, prayed that she did, but also wondered if he could handle it.

When her breath touched the base, he knew he wasn't going to be able to. "You do what I think you're about to do I must warn you." He panted. "I won't have any control."

She picked his cock up and stroked it, looking at him from between his legs. "Good."

Drakon fisted his hands into the sheets, watching her open her mouth and take the head of his cock inside. He lost his breath with the sucking of it in, the feel of her hot tongue on the underside. He could tell by her movements that she was unsure of what she was doing, but didn't give a damn. To him, it was heaven and the best but it was also going to be very, very short with the way she pulled and sucked on him.

"Amelia," he panted. "For sake of the gods, slow down or I'm going to lose it real fast." Her answer to him was a moan that vibrated all around his cock. "Son of a bitch!"

It was coming and coming so fast he couldn't even think about pushing it back. Drakon closed his eyes, put a fist in his mouth, and came with a rush. It was heaven and it was hell at the same time.

She slid up his body, kissing as she went. Drakon worked to get his breathing under control, but the more he fought it the stronger his desire and lust became. When she was up to his chest he moved, changing positioned and flipping her to back her stomach. He got her up to her knees and in one fluid motion was burned to his balls inside her.

Amelia was a tight fit, and he loved it. He moved inside her, stroked the inner muscles, and teased the ring of her ass with his fingers. He brought back juices from her pussy as he lunged inside her.

Their bodies slapped against each other and the room filled up with the sweet scent of their lovemaking. Drakon felt possessed. He took her hard and fast, pounded into her with a need he never felt before.

Amelia cried out and fell forward. Drakon went on, pumping into her, teasing her ass. He moved one of her arms and put her hand under her body. He showed her how to play with her swollen clit while he kept moving.

"Come again, Amelia," he said in her ear. "Milk my cock. Make me come." He groaned, closing his eyes when she tightened around him. "Yeah, just like that," he moaned.

He swelled inside her and blew. Drakon arched back and panted loudly, his cock contracted his release. It left him spent, yet still hungry and, surprisingly, still hard. Wrapping his arms around her, he flipped over to his back, taking her with him.

Drakon parted the globes of her ass, put the head of his cock against the tight ring, and just waited for her to understand what he wanted.

"Tell me no, and I'll stop," he said, breathing hard.

Amelia shifted on him, coming to her knees with legs parted. Her hands went to his legs and she bent forward a bit. "I want to experience this," she told him.

He took a deep breath and lowered her to him. She was wet enough back there, but unused. No one had ever touched her back here, and the ring didn't seem to want to give for him.

"I don't want to hurt you," he said. He took hold of his cock and rubbed it back and forth then tried to help press it into her.

"Do it." She groaned, pushing back against him. "I don't care about the pain. I just want to feel you inside me."

Licking his lips, Drakon held his cock firmly so he wouldn't hurt himself and with her help coming back against him, he forced the head into her. It was hard, but it finally gave with a pop, and Amelia cried out. He stopped, or at least tried to, but she kept pushing back against him, lowering herself.

Drakon had his mouth open, he breathed or was trying to breathe through it while he felt one of the tightest places ever stretch and part for him. Fully embedded into her ass, he struggled to breath. It was a task he found he could barely do and it didn't help that she moved on him, grinded a little and moved his hand between her legs.

"Do this real easy now," he told her. "Slowly move."

However, she didn't move slowly. She barely removed him from her and slammed back down. He moaned and she whimpered. Drakon had hoped that this position might be better for her since it gave her the control, but control for the first time might not be the best in her hands. So again, he moved them, only this time he moved her to the edge of the bed, and he stood up.

Slowly he pulled out, leaving the head in, and slowly he slid back in. He did this several times and touched her clit a few of those strokes as well. Within seconds, she was relaxed and he was moving steadily into her.

"Faster," Amelia panted softly. With each stroke into her a breathless sound came from her.

"I go any faster I'm going to come quickly."

She shook her head. "I don't care, just move fast. Please!"

Drakon bit his lower lip and picked up the speed. He moaned and she pushed back. He lunged into her as fast as he could, fighting the pressure that was building inside him.

"Don't stop!" she moaned with in a high pitch. "Oh, God, don't stop!"

Amelia bit down on the covers and cried out. He felt her orgasm and came with her. He kept stroking her as his seed came out, but it left him weak. He tumbled to the floor and she kept on her feet. He was still coming on the floor, powerless to stop it.

She also dropped to the floor, resting her head on his arm. Both breathed fast and hard and Drakon kept thinking and wondering if he had the energy to do it again.

"Will every time be like that?" she asked.

"By the gods, I hope so," he panted. "I want to feel like I've died each time we're together."

Morning came all too soon for her. Amelia stood next to her window, watching the sunrise. Drakon left only an hour before it came. He made love to her three more times and she was sore in all the right places from it. Her body still tingled for it and hungered for more but she couldn't rest in his arms or enjoy it for too long. Her servant would be here to help bath and dress her for another day.

Kyril threatened her home and her people if she didn't marry him. There was no point in telling Corydon. He wouldn't believe her. He'd think she was only trying to get out of a marriage and needed to give the peace treaty a chance. Yet deep down she couldn't give him a chance. She knew what he was and agreed with Drakon. Kyril wouldn't be satisfied with peace; he would start a war in Egypt or drain it dry.

Drakon asked her to keep the game going until his men arrived. She needed to act the maiden of the house and let Kyril court her for the new few days until the wedding. If the men didn't show by then, Drakon was going to sneak her out, just like Alexis had done with his son.

Could she last that long? Only if Drakon was able to come to her each night, but he couldn't. Already he took a big chance by coming last night. If they were discovered, he could be put to death and Kyril would turn her into his whore.

"My Lady?"

Her servants arrived. Amelia hugged herself tighter. "A hot bath please."

"Yes, My Lady. And Lord Kyril has sent this."

She turned to see her ladies holding a gown that didn't belong to her. A dark red dress to match the necklace he gave her with a gray fur wrap that had black speckles in it.

"He has requested very strongly that you wear it today for the feast, along with the jewel he gave."

Her heart sank. To wear this would be to show everyone that she was indeed going to marry him. What would Drakon say or do once he saw her in this? She almost cringed at the thought.

"What did Corydon say?"

Her servant looked almost ashamed. "He assured Lord Kyril that you would be in it and was honored to show respect to the Prince of Drystal's tradition as well."

Is that so! "I think it's time the maiden of the house shows both how she's going to act to this arrangement. My style."

They all smiled at her. "Yes, My Lady."

The dress was handed off to one of the other servants, and the one that spoke went over to her closet, pulling out one of the new dresses she had yet to wear. A long, flowing blue dress was placed on the bed. It slipped over her shoulders, had sleeves, but over the shoulders was bare. It flowed to the ground, no slits but did have a bare back where gold chains hung down in U-shapes. Her hair, after it was washed and dried, was curled tight, then a matching blue pearl hair band slid over her head, keeping the hair from her face and forehead. Soft slippers were places on her feet as were thick gold bands around her wrists.

She looked at herself in the mirror once her maids were finished and had to smile. She did look like the maiden of the house. "Perfect. Now let's go greet the day."

* * * *

Kyril sat at the table waiting for Amelia to show for the morning meal. He was a bit anxious to see her in her wedding dress and became instantly pissed when she walked inside dressed not in the one he sent. He thought they had an understanding. Apparently, he was mistaken.

"Watch her eyes," Ismame told him while she rode him like a stallion. "You can read so much from my dear sister by her eyes. I bet she's given herself to someone else."

Kyril did watch Amelia closely. He saw the slight glance she sent to Drakon and Alexis and it had him wondering if she was right about her sister. *Have you given my prize away to another?* Was she truly the maiden that she claimed to be? If he went and accused her of it, and it turned out to be his mistake, it could damage the game he was playing. Then, what if she isn't all she claimed to be?

Amelia didn't sit next to him as he expected. Instead, she sat down next to her brother, eyes forward. He thought that if she was indeed without the treasure he sought, and then she sure was playing it up as if it was still there.

Ismame was the last to show up. She glided in and sat down across from her husband, a big smile on her face. Kyril inwardly smiled. After she pleased him with her mouth, he really worked her over hard. It surprised him some with how well she took it, and how easy it was to sodomize her, expecting to shock her, expecting it to not be easy. But he soon realized that Alexis' wife had definitely been shown the rough side of bed sport. By the time, he was finished with her she could barely walk from the room. Kyril was crossing his fingers that sweet Amelia would be able to handle his various appetites like her sister. If not, well then he would enjoy teaching her.

The meal ended up being longer that what he would've liked but Kyril bared it. He watched everyone. Saw how Drakon and Alexis behaved, catching the glances that Amelia cast towards them. The longer he sat there observing, the more he suspected that indeed something was going on with Amelia and one of those men.

Once the meal finished, Kyril followed Amelia from the room without drawing any attention. He caught up with her easily since he was pretty sure she thought he would stay and drink or go with Corydon. He caught her by the arm, kept walking, and ignoring her attempts to pull away from him.

"It isn't proper for you to be dragging me like this," she said.

He took her all the way back to his own chamber, shoving her inside and slamming the doors closed. Kyril stood in front of the door, blocking her from leaving until he was ready.

"Was I not clear about the dress and necklace?" he asked, crossing his arms over his chest.

Her chest rose and fell, nostrils flared and eyes narrowed on him. She was pissed. Good! It meant she had passion inside her and fight.

"I don't take well to being threatened," she said.

"Oh, when I extend a threat, you'll know it."

She also crossed her arms over her chest. "Are you threatening me?"

"If I was, then my dear you would know it." He almost found humor in her anger. What he did enjoy was the fire in her eyes and couldn't wait to sample it.

"There are some things in Egypt that I hold dear to my heart, some tradition that I feel shouldn't be broken. And wearing a wedding dress before the wedding is one of them."

"Is that so?"

"Yes."

"And does that mean you wish to have the bedding witnessed then, since it's a tradition for royal houses to prove the innocence of the maiden? Because I was thinking of keeping that between us."

"You assume there is going to be a wedding."

Kyril laughed right before he charged her. He backed Amelia up to the far wall where he boxed her in. That fire in her eyes quickly turned into fear and both turned him on.

"The safety of your home and people rests on your shoulders," he informed her. "Do you wish to test to see how serious I am?"

"Another threat?" She batted her eyes up at him. "Why does that not surprise me?"

"Oh, it isn't a threat." He reached up, brushing the back of his hand across her cheek. "I never make threats."

She slapped his hand away and ducked under his arm. "I don't care for the liberties you take. I don't belong to you." She turned, her chin up. "You have no right to touch me."

"As your husband to be, I have every right." He pushed away from the wall and slowly advanced toward her. "If I desired, I could bed you right now, as my right." She kept backing away from him and if he wasn't mistaken, he saw a slight tremor go through her. "As your intended, I am entitled to many liberties, and I think I intend to take one right now!" Kyril rushed her, slamming his hands on the door over her head once more. She jumped, blinking several times.

"What are you talking about?" she breathed out, the fear showing in her eyes.

He licked his lips and purposely roamed her body with his eyes. "I'm talking about seeing what truly belongs to me." He grabbed the front of her dress and ripped it, exposing her breasts.

Amelia screamed and he stopped, staring down at her. Kyril didn't attack her like she thought he would but instead took two steps backwards, still staring at her, his face paling slightly. He said nothing. When he moved again she flinched, waiting for another attack, but instead he pushed her away from the door, slid the bolt back and left as fast as he could.

Not sure what to do, Amelia covered her chest as best she could, and it was then that she knew what had him stopping his attack. Love bites on her breast.

"Oh God!" she gasped, her eyes widening. Holding the ripped front of her dress to her breasts, Amelia left the room at a run, back to her own room where she could change and collect herself. Lord only knew what was going to happen next.

Chapter Six

Corydon busted into Amelia bedchamber just as she slipped into her robe. She jumped, turned, and looked at him with wide eyes.

"Out!" he ordered her maids. Behind him stood the doctor and two of his guards.

"Corydon, what's going on?"

"Kyril came to see me." His eyes narrowed on her. He didn't advance towards her, just stood by the door. "Seems to think that you're not what you seem."

"I don't understand."

"Oh but I think you do," he sneered. "He informed me that he saw something on you that shouldn't be there." A snap of his fingers and the men that joined him walked around Corydon and up to her, taking hold of her arms.

Kyril entered then, another woman with him. "Ah, I see you've beaten me to it."

"I have this under control, Kyril," Corydon said through his teeth.

"I'm sure you don't," Kyril said, his eyes on Amelia. "In any case, I've brought my own servant to make sure things go, shall we say smoothly."

"Will someone please tell me what the hell is going on?" Amelia demanded, trying to get out of the hold the men had on her.

"I'm demanding a test." Kyril smiled at her. "I need reassurance that you are what you say you are."

Amelia looked at him as if he'd lost his mind. "A test! What kind of test?" Her gut screamed that whatever it was it wasn't going to be good. Not by a long shot!

She was dragged from the room, Kyril right behind her with the midwife. Amelia looked over her shoulder and saw that Corydon and Drakon were also following them.

"The one that will prove you are as you say," Kyril answered, turning to nod to the woman next to him. "It's time to see if your still the maiden or not."

"What?" she gasped, fighting the hold the men had on her. "Kyril you can't do this!"

"But I can." Kyril said. "It's my right to assure myself that all is as it should be which means I'm questioning your virtue."

"I told you I'd handle this," Corydon said.

"And I'm only making sure you do," Kyril snapped back. "Do it."

"Corydon, if you allow this to happen, then I'll refuse him at the altar!" she yelled, fighting the men as they took her over to the bed. Amelia knew if it her lack of virginity was discovered, then war could break out right now. She didn't fear for herself but for Drakon.

"Do it," Corydon snapped.

Amelia was shoved down on the bed; the men went over her head, holding her arms up while the doctor and the woman stood down by her legs. They parted her legs and the woman touched her first, then the doctor. Both put only one finger inside her. Tears came to her eyes knowing that very soon all hell was about to break lose.

The exam only took seconds, but it felt like a lifetime. It was over in three deep breaths, her dress lowered, and everyone let her go. She sat up, but kept her head down as they both walked over to Corydon and Kyril. Kyril didn't say a word. He left the room, slamming the door closed.

"Out," Corydon ordered.

Amelia began to shake in her fear. She clasped her hands together on her lap; head still hung down and waited. She wasn't sure what he would say or do to her now that they were alone. Just like, she didn't know what she was going to tell him. If she told him the truth, that she gave herself willingly to Drakon, then a war could break out between Egypt and Corinth, maybe even Rome as well since Drakon was Alexis' right hand man. As things stood now Drystal could also rage in betrayal. They took arrange marriages very seriously, and it was stated clearly in the contract that Kyril was to marry the maiden of the house.

Corydon walked towards her, his boots echoing so loudly in the quiet room. He stopped in front of her, and it took all of her willpower to move her eyes from his boots up to his face. One blink and the back of his hand connected with her face.

Amelia cried out, falling to her right side on the bed. Corydon grabbed her arm brutally, forced her to her feet, and slapped her again on the same side before shoving her away from him. She landed on the floor hard, knocking the breath out of her.

"How could you do this to me!" he yelled. "How could you shame me like this? Do you have any idea what you've done?"

"I didn't do this to hurt you," she shook her head as she cried.

He rushed her, kneeling down, taking hold of her face. The anger Amelia saw in his eyes had her cringing. "Don't you understand? You've ruined us!" He shoved her away and stood back up. "You would've had anything you ever wanted, married to Kyril. Now you're fit for nothing more than being his whore!"

She sniffed back the fresh tears and stood up slowly. "I'll never let him touch me," she seethed. "I hate him!" she screamed.

Corydon slapped her again, knocking her back down to the ground. "You'll do as I tell you." He bent over, fisting his hand into her hair. "Who was it? Who was the bastard that you ruined you?"

Amelia shook her head. "I'll never tell you."

"Oh, you will tell me. Guards!" he yelled, bringing the men back. "Take her to the table."

"Corydon no!" Amelia screamed, fear gripping her.

The table was the punishment room. One was strapped down on the stomach, the backside bared for a whipping. Only once in her life did she ever see it used and that was by their father. What the woman that had been whipped had done, she had no idea, but their father had all three of his children there to witness it to keep them all in line. It worked! Not one of them ever got out of line with their father for fear of the table. Never in her whole life did she think that her brother would use this on her.

"Then give me his name!" he yelled again, his face getting red.

Again, she shook her head, "I can't."

"Take her."

They grabbed her by the arms, picking her up, dragging her from the room. "Corydon please!" she sobbed, unable to find the strength to fight.

"Corydon!"

* * * *

"We have to go now!" Alexis busted into Drakon's chambers, his men, and servants right behind him. The servants went to work packing up things.

"What's wrong?" he jumped up from his desk, watched while his clothes were shoved into bags, not packed.

"Kyril demanded Amelia tested for her virtue. She failed." Alexis met Drakon's eyes. "But then, you'd know she would fail."

"What?"

"Kyril's already left the palace and Corydon is punishing Amelia into finding the one that ruined her." Alexis picked up Drakon's jacket and tossed it to him. "I doubt she'll last very long and Ismame has left. I have no fucking idea where she went."

"The hell he is!" Drakon rushed to the door, only to have Alexis stop him by grabbing hold of him.

"Think, damn it!" he yelled in Drakon's face. "You go in there and you're both dead." He shook Drakon "You want to save her then you have to get out of here to do it. You need to meet up with your men before Kyril has a chance to get reinforcements."

As much as Drakon hated the idea of leaving Amelia here, Alexis had a point. "Alright, let's go."

However, it wasn't to be that easy. Right when they rounded the first hallway they met up with Corydon's men and, from the look of things, Amelia had talked. They were armed and ready to fight, which pleased Drakon very much.

He withdrew his sword, as did Alexis. Only five came to arrest him and five they put to the ground hard. Before leaving, Drakon bent over and picked one up by the front of his shirt, bringing his face close to his own.

"Take this back to Corydon," he growled. "I will be back, and there's going to hell with me." A punch and the man was out cold.

Horses were waiting for them and they all didn't hesitate to jump on the backs, kicking them into a run. They rode the whole way to the substation, not stopping at all, and each mile they passed tore at Drakon's heart. Right when the substation came into view, he stopped his horse, unable to go further.

"Drakon?" Alexis asked.

Breathing hard, Drakon shook his head. "I can't. I can't leave her."

"We'll come back."

"I can't Alexis, I'm sorry." He turned his horse and urged him forward, leaving Alexis.

"Drakon!" Alexis yelled after him.

* * * *

Kyril sat in the middle of his war tent, drumming fingers on the wooden arm, his anger slowly rising with each second that he waited. He set up only two miles from the city, in the dessert and sent word to his father that the maiden of the house wasn't pure. He also sent in his message that Egypt would burn for this betrayal and that Amelia would become his slave. His father sent back a message only five minutes ago giving his blessing. Egypt was about to burn.

He heard the sound of horses coming fast. Standing up, Kyril walked out of the tent and stood in front of the entrance watching as two horses were coming toward the camp quickly, dark cloaks flapping out around the riders. Around him, the men were still setting things up and fires burned all over with pots cooking over them. Others were sharpening swords, getting arrows ready and a few making sure the lasers they snuck in were charged and ready for use.

The riders stopped in front of him and the one in the lead pushed back the hood on the cloak. Ismame smiled down at him.

"My lord," she said.

"Ismame," Kyril acknowledged her. "I have to say, I'm a bit shocked to see you. What have you brought me so soon?"

"Oh many things," she swung her leg over the horse and slid down to the ground. It was then he saw the rope she held. With a jerk, the one on the other horse fell to the ground. "And I'm sure you'll like it all."

She walked to the one that fell and yanked the cloak off from the head, revealing Amelia, tied and gaged. She had dark circles around her eyes and looked a bit pale.

"Oh, do tell how you got ahold of her," Kyril said, smiling big.

"Let's just say my brother left her alone after the punishment," Ismame smiled back.

"And your brother?"

"He won't be bothering you, trust me."

"Otho!" Kyril called out. One man from the group gathered around stepped forward. He was about as large as Kyril but not built as solid. He had the same cold eyes as the rest of the men. "Take my new pet and have her dressed for her new role. Ismame, come and join me. I'm dying to hear what you've done for your kingdom."

* * * *

Drakon pulled the horse to a stop in front of the palace steps and looked in horror at the sight before him. Bodies lined the steps, blood everywhere. He swung from the horse, pulled his sword, and started a slow walk up. Behind him, he heard Alexis stop and jump from his house.

"What the hell happened?" Alexis asked.

"I don't know."

Inside, there was more proof of a battle. More bodies, lots more blood and a few fires burned. Clearly, something major happened right after they left, and from the looks of things, Corydon's side didn't appear to have won the battle.

Drakon followed the trail of bodies all the way to the throne room where he saw a sight that he never thought he'd see. Corydon slumped in the chair, blood covering his body.

Drakon rushed to him, dropping to his knees before him. "Corydon!"

Corydon opened his eyes, opened his mouth, and then rolled off the chair to the floor. Drakon managed to catch his head before it banged on the stone floor.

"She betrayed us," Corydon panted. "Never thought she'd do this."

"Who?" Drakon asked. Corydon's breathing got faster and his eyes closed. Drakon knew it was only a matter of time before the man died. "Corydon, where's Amelia?"

Corydon's eyes opened, that half focused on Drakon. "She never gave you up. Gods forgive me for what I've done to her," he whispered as blood came out of his mouth and he coughed.

"Where is she?" Drakon tried again.

"I don't know," he sighed, eyes closing again, shaking his head. "Ismame took her."

"Ismame!" Alexis said.

"She did this," Corydon went on, his eyes opening again. This time he grabbed the front of Drakon's shirt, jerking him close. Where he got the strength, Drakon didn't know. "You are the one to save us."

A fog seemed to go right over his eyes and his last breath touched Drakon's face. Corydon, Pharaoh of Egypt was dead.

"My lord."

Both him and Alexis turned, swords back in their hands, readying for a fight, stilled when they saw one of Amelia's maids standing in the doorway. Her white dress had blood on it, was ripped, and from the bruises on her body and the way her face looked, it was clear she had been raped and most likely left for dead.

"Did Ismame do this?" Alexis asked.

"She let some of Lord Kyril's men into the palace. They killed everyone they could find and used us." Fresh tears filled her eyes, spilled down her cheeks. "They left me for dead."

"Amelia?"

"Ismame took her to Kyril," she sniffed.

"Then I go after Kyril," Drakon stated.

Alexis grabbed his arm, stopping him. "You need the men to go after Kyril. I'm sure by now he has an army with him and we're outnumbered. We need to stop and think here."

He was right. Drakon decided Alexis knew what he was talking about, after all, he led them in battle many times, and they always came out winners.

"How could Ismame do this?" Drakon asked. Looking around at all the dead men. "How could she turn her back on her family and team up with Kyril?"

"Ismame has always wanted the throne," Alexis said. "Guess now she thinks she can have it with Kyril's help."

"Why the hell didn't we see this side of her?"

Drakon left the hall, the maid and Alexis following him.

"I think we did, we just didn't think that side was this bad."

* * * *

Kyril took a step back from the bed and from Ismame who was face down. He'd used her hard and well, for hours, sating not only the lust that built up from seeing and being close to Amelia, but the anger and learning of her betrayal. He used Ismame until she was bleeding, and still he used her until she begged him for no more. Now she was on her stomach, crying and his sheets were red from her blood.

His anger, for the moment had mellowed and he could think about his own kind of punishment for Amelia for her deceiving him into thinking that he would get a pure bride. Even now, she was being dressed for his pleasure. He also was told that her brother whipped her for the betrayal with the hopes of learning who it was that took his prize. She didn't give up a name, but he didn't need one. He had a pretty good idea he knew the man that took what rightfully belonged to him.

He snapped his finger the moment he stepped from the thin curtain that separated the bed from the rest of the tent. A female servant he took from the palace quickly came over to him, dropped down to her knees with a cup in hand, and head down. He took the drink and stood there for her to clean his body of blood. Before she was done, the tent opened and one of his men came inside. Kyril grabbed his robe, motioned for the girl to leave him, and took a seat in the only chair he had in the tent.

"Was she good?" Otho asked with a nod to Ismame, putting a large green grape in his mouth when he moved around the table with food.

"Better now that I don't have to put on a show." Kyril grinned, "Would you care to try for yourself?"

Otho smiled, "I might. Only after, she has healed from you. I like to feel the tear, just as much as you do."

Kyril chuckled. "Then maybe we should have her together. I doubt she has experienced two cocks at the same time."

Otho happened to be his half, bastard brother. After Kyril's mother died, his father sought his pleasures from a mistress he stopped seeing for a very long time. He promised the woman marriage if she gave him another son, but died after his birth. Otho was raised as Kyril's brother and had the same cruel appetite.

"Your Amelia is ready," Otho said, popping another grape into his mouth. "Will you be sharing her also?"

Looking at Otho was like looking in a mirror. "Maybe after I've fucked this need out of my system. I swear I've never wanted a woman as much as her. Lucky for me also, I don't have to be a loving husband now. Since she's no longer a virgin I can use her as I please and as hard."

Otho took a deep breath and picked up a cup. He poured himself some wine then moved to the door, staring out. "Drakon's men have landed and are heading for the palace. Without having men in the palace we won't know what they are planning."

"Oh I have a pretty good idea what they are planning." Otho looked over his shoulder at Kyril. "Drakon wants her. He's already had a taste. Hell, I won't even put it past the bastard to think he's in love with her."

Otho turned fully around, meeting Kyril in the eyes. "Love is a very powerful weapon, just like an obsession, which has me worried for you, my brother. It isn't healthy to want a woman the way you want her. It's a weakness that can be used against you."

"I'll remember that next time you desire a woman."

Otho snickered and took a drink. "So when will we make our attack?"

"As soon as the men are ready," Kyril sighed. "They need to have their pleasures first, and have been very good with waiting for us to return."

Otho nodded, turned, and put his cup down on a near table. "You don't want to give them too much of a leave. They still need to fight."

"Yes, but without the pleasure of women we won't get much out of them now." Kyril laughed. "I did get all of the women that were left in the palace after all, so let him have their fun. They can fuck for a few hours then fight."

"Then come dawn we fight?"

Taking a deep breath, Kyril stood up. "Dawn we fight. Now, brother, if you'll excuse me, I think I'll go and see my new toy. Feel free to enjoy Ismame while I'm gone. I'm sure she's more than ready for another round and once you're done, let the men have what's left. I'm finished with her."

Otho smiled and moved towards the bed. Kyril also smiled, dropped his robe to get dressed, and had his pants back on when Ismame cried out. He almost envied his brother at the moment, but then thought about the one that awaited him, the one that he hungered for above all else.

* * * *

"Amelia!"

Amelia turned her head towards her mother. Basilia of Egypt, Queen, grabbed her youngest daughter and ran the second their home was broken into. Amelia did not know where her sister or brother went or her father. All she knew was when her mother grabbed her she held on tightly.

They were now hiding in the barn. Basilia was trying to get hold of a horse so they could go to the safe house. They all were to go there.

Her brother screamed and Amelia put herself into a large pile of hay. She peaked out to see her mother struggling with a man, or more like a boy the same age as her brother.

He hit her on the side of her head. Basilia went down, and Amelia covered her mouth to silence the crying. Her mother was then dragged by her hair to an empty stale. Amelia heard ripping of clothes, more slapping, and then the cry from her mother and grunting from the man.

Amelia snapped out of her thoughts when the flaps of the tent opened, and Kyril in the flesh stood there. She wanted to cross her arms over the scaly dressed outfit he had forced her to wear, but couldn't.

The clothing, if it could be even called that, barely covered her. A gold band twisted around her breasts, barely covering the mounds and went around her shoulders and back. The skirt was made of the same material around her waist that weaved around her hips with one long piece of cloth between her legs and another hanging down to cover her ass. Both legs were completely bare and she had a thick gold collar around her neck that had chains going down to connect to her wrists. Her hair was braided in several tiny braids then twisted together to flow down the center of her back.

She looked like a whore, which she suspected was how he wanted her to look.

"Out," he told the ones guarding her. Amelia stood up to face him, refusing to be on the ground. "You could have had it all, if you only kept your legs closed." He walked inside and slowly strolled around her, touching her hair, a finger to her shoulder. "Could've been queen."

"No thank you."

"I know who he is," he went on. "I'm not stupid. I've seen the way you looked at him when we dined."

"Where's Ismame?"

"Oh, getting hers. I can't very well have someone who would stab her brother in the back working by my side now." He stopped in front of her. "No, that traitorous bitch is better used on her back."

Amelia spit in his face. "You disgust me."

He smiled and wiped his face, "Oh how I'm going to enjoy breaking you." The hand came fast and swift. Contact to her cheek and she went down to the ground, stunned. "I think the first lesson I'm going to teach you is control. After all, I can't have my slave back-talking the way you like; it shows a lack of respect."

He reached behind his back and brought out a whip. Amelia refused to show him an ounce of fear. "Beat me all you want, Kyril, but you'll never get my respect or loyalty."

"We shall see."

* * * *

Kyril walked back to his own tent, whistling and smiling. "Otho, you done?" he called out once inside. "I think I might need another turn. Looks as if Amelia needs a few lessons before I can ride her. Man she is going to be so much fun to break."

Kyril went to a table and poured himself a drink, tossing the whip he brought back aside. He also grabbed a chunk of meat and took a bite, enjoying everything at the moment. The food tasted great, the wine sweet as ever. Hell, even the tent felt comfortable at the moment. He was on a high and nothing could bring it down.

"Oh let me tell you, brother, the outfit you picked for her was perfect." He had his back to the bedding area and started to undress with a smile. "I loved how those cups fit over her breasts. Since she wants to play the whore to another, she now has the right clothing for the task."

124

After pulling his shirt from the waist, he moved to the large pitcher of water, pouring some in the bowl to wash his hands. "And I must say the whipping went well. Didn't even break the skin, but she will feel it come morning. Are you listening to me?" He looked over his shoulder. Otho hadn't moved.

Kyril looked closer through the curtain. Otho was laying spread out on the bed, Ismame not there. "Did you give her to the men then? Was she not to your liking?"

Nothing but silence greeted him.

"Otho?" With a frown, Kyril walked to the bed, pushed the curtains aside and looked in completely shocked. Otho lay on the bed dead, this throat slit. "You bitch!" he yelled, turned away from the scene and grabbed his knife, dashing back out of the tent.

* * * *

Ismame rushed into the tent that Amelia was being held in, bloody knife in hand. What she saw had her wanting to cry in shame. Amelia lay on the ground, on her stomach, her backside raw and red from another beating.

"Oh, Amelia, I'm so sorry!" Ismame covered her mouth and rushed to her sister. "Forgive me." She cut the rope that held the chain and helped Amelia to her feet.

"Ismame?" Amelia sound broken. "What're you doing here?"

"Come on, we're getting out of here." Ismame pretty much had to carry Amelia out of the tent, but she didn't mind. She thought by letting Kyril's men kill Corydon and giving herself to him that she would get the throne of Egypt, but instead, what she got was pain and regret. "This was not how it was supposed to happen."

"What did you do?" Amelia asked once they were outside.

"You don't want to know, trust me. Because if I could, I'd forget it all and go back to before this nightmare ever started. Gods help me, I wish I could go back."

Chapter Seven

Amelia ran with what little energy she had left. The pain in her body excruciating. She pushed through it, pushed and ran with her sister towards freedom and help.

Ismame snuck her out of the camp. How she did it, Amelia couldn't say, and what Ismame had done that she kept asking the gods to forgive her for, she wouldn't say. Amelia feared the worst and deep down knew the worst happened.

Corydon was dead.

It's the only explanation for why Kyril had the balls to set up camp and prepare for war, not to mention treating her as he had. Whipping her, dressing her like a whore, not all of it would have happened if Corydon weren't dead.

"Ismame, I've got to stop," Amelia, begged, unable to keep making her legs move or catch her breath. She didn't just stop finally; she dropped down to the sand, gasping for all the air she could get into her lungs.

"We can't stop," Ismame said, also breathing hard. "By now I'm sure Kyril has found what I've done and is going to be after us."

"What did you do?"

"Come on, we have to keep going," Ismame helped Amelia back to her feet, holding most of her weight for her.

"Where're we going?"

"To the camp. I'm sure Alexis and Drakon have set up by now and are getting ready themselves to fight Kyril."

"Why are you doing this?" She couldn't figure her sister out. Nothing Ismame ever did made any sense to her. One second she would be loving and caring, then in the next stab you in the back if it would further her cause.

"I made a mistake," Ismame answered. "A very big one."

"Tell me."

They only went a short distance before stopping again. Amelia welcomed the break. She needed it. Lying on her side since her back burned from the whippings she received not only by Corydon but by Kyril also. Every move she made had it feeling like it was ten times worse than what it should be. She could only imagine what the bruising looked like. Thinking about the pleasure that Kyril got from the act sent chills down her spine. She just thanked the gods that he didn't rape her once he was finished.

"I thought with Kyril's help I could overthrow our brother," Ismame said. "I let the men into the palace. While they kept the guards busy, and Corydon, I went in and took you away. It was the price he asked for, if I wanted the crown."

"Oh, Ismame," Amelia sighed.

"But it all went wrong." tears filled Ismame's eyes and fell down. "I went to bed with Kyril once and it was great, but the second time he was brutal to me." She sniffed and more fell. "He did things to me that I never in my worst nightmares thought a man could do," she whispered then and wiped the falling tears away. "Then he gave me to his brother to use and I found out that while I was bringing you here, Kyril had ordered Corydon killed. Our brother is dead and it's all my fault."

* * * *

"What are you doing?" Alexis asked.

Drakon worked fast at saddling his horse. They caught up with the men, briefed them quickly, and then planned the best possible course of action for attack. He sent out a scout who informed them that Kyril had men and from the looks of things, they were camping there for at least the time Kyril happened to be staying in the palace. That told Drakon that Kyril was planning to attack all along, just as he thought. A shame that Corydon had to find this out the hard way.

"I'm going to find Amelia," he answered Alexis, tightened the strap one last time before swinging himself up on the back.

"We're not ready yet."

"I am."

"Drakon, think!" Alexis grabbed hold of the reins before Drakon could turn the horse around and leave. "You go to his camp without backup and you won't come out of this alive."

"I'm not going to sit here and let that bastard have his way with her. Gods alone knows what he's done or is doing to her even now."

"But you're not thinking."

"Damn it, Alexis, I am!" he yelled, jerking the reins free. "I'm more focused than ever on what I need to do. If I can get her out and to safety then I won't have to worry about her when we attack. I wait, and then I'm going to be distracted."

"Shit," Alexis sighed. "Well at least let me go with you for backup."

"No," he said as he turned the horse. "You have the men ready for attack at sunset. I don't want these fuckers here any longer. They die tonight." With a nudge, the horse shot off, leaving dust behind him.

* * * *

"Ismame stop!" Amelia cried out, the burning in her side becoming so unbearable she dropped to the sand. "I can't go further."

Ismame breathed hard and fast. She stopped and turned back to Amelia. "We have to keep going. We're just about there."

However, Amelia couldn't seem to get her legs to move. She shook her head. "I can't."

The sun beat down on them all day, making the trip on foot ten times harder than if they were on horses but with the two beatings, the sun burning her flesh and no water, Amelia feared she was done for. She just couldn't move.

Ismame walked back to her, bent over to help Amelia back on her feet, and stopped. Amelia saw her sister's face pale and had to look over her shoulder as well to see what it might be she saw. A single rider coming towards them fast.

"Run," Ismame ordered.

It was such a task, such a struggle to get back up on her feet, but with Ismame's help, she did it, only she couldn't move just yet.

"Ismame?"

"Run!" Ismame gave her a push, and Amelia nearly went back down on the hot sand. Only when the rider got closer did Amelia see whom it was.

Kyril!

Ismame headed towards him, and somehow Amelia was able to get her legs to move. She took off running, only to stop and watch to see what her sister might do. She ran right at the horse, screaming and waving her hands in the air, scaring the horse so bad it reared up on his legs, knocking Kyril right off.

"Ismame!" Amelia screamed.

"Run!" Ismame yelled back.

Kyril stood up, unsheathed his sword, and stabbed it through Ismame's chest.

"Ismame! No!" Amelia screamed again.

He pulled back and her sister slumped to the ground. Amelia couldn't move. She was rooted to the spot, staring at her fallen sister and the man who just killed her; the man that her brother tried to give to not too long again. Only when his eyes moved up to her—those cold eyes—was she able to get her legs to move. He grabbed part of Ismame's dress, cleaned the sword off, and slowly began to walk towards her.

Amelia shook her head, turned and ran. She ignored the pain in her side, in her back and the burn the sand caused to her bare feet. She ignored it all, and just focused on getting away, on running as fast as she could from this man.

She heard him following her, heard the heavy breathing and the deep imprints in the sand behind her, and it helped her to move faster. It also helped her to go into a panic.

A scream left her lips when his hands went around her hair, yanking her hard to a stop and back into his brutal arms, but the hold didn't last for long. To the right of them a horse whinnied and Amelia was shoved away. She had a second to look to the right, saw a rider and a horse that was up on its hind legs, hooves in the air. She rolled clear mere seconds before it came down.

Drakon sat on the horse.

"Drakon," she breathed out, scooting even farther away from the horse and Kyril.

"Let's finish this, Kyril," Drakon swung one leg over and jumped from the back of the horse. "For good."

"Yes, lets," Kyril smiled, pulling his sword back out of its sheath.

Drakon did as well.

She stayed on the ground, unable to move, just sat there watching as the two men began to circle around each other, waiting for the other to strike first.

Kyril was the first. He swung high, coming down hard, and Drakon blocked it, countered it with a shove and a swung his own. Sparks flew with each hard contact blade made to blade.

Back and forth, left, and right, the steel clashed, sparks flying and the clashing seemed to echo in the open dessert. All Amelia could do was sit on the ground; watching and praying to the Gods Drakon came out of this alive.

Kyril swung wide and low causing Drakon to jump back, slightly bent. Kyril then swung again, this time with his fist, hitting Drakon in the face, drawing first blood. She gasped, covering her mouth with both hands.

"I'm going to enjoy watching you bleed," Kyril, sneered. "Just as you enjoyed taking what was by right mine!"

"She's never going to be yours," Drakon sneered back, his chest rising and falling quickly.

Two steps and Drakon bore his sword down on Kyril. This time when Kyril blocked it his legs buckled under him and he went down on one knee. Drakon pressed down with what looked like his whole body weight. How Kyril managed to hold him off, she couldn't say, but the sight had her holding her breath, waiting to see who would come out of this alive.

With a yell, Kyril pushed Drakon off and took a swing. Drakon blocked it and hit him back with the fist that held the hilt of his sword. Kyril yelled out, blood from his nose running down his face.

"I'll kill you!" Kyril yelled.

Kyril swung like a wild man and still Drakon blocked it, but not without taking a couple steps backward. Kyril began to pound at Drakon's sword, yelling the whole time, sounding crazed. The blows had Drakon to his knees, fending him off the best he could.

Amelia began to get scared then. She feared that Kyril might win and feared what he would do to her also. She stood up, swaying on her feet, trying to keep her balance and ignoring the pain. She went over to Drakon's horse, took one of his daggers from the saddlebags. Making her way around to the backside of Kyril, Amelia struck him in the back with it, shoving the blade in as deep as she could.

Kyril stopped pounding on Drakon and yelled, his sword dropping to the ground and both hands reaching around his back. "You bitch!" He swung around, hitting her hard across the face, knocking her down as well.

Amelia landed hard, the wind knocked out of her. She stayed on the ground, belly down, looking over her shoulder while Kyril tried to reach the knife in his back. She tasted blood in the inside of mouth from his hit, but didn't move. The distraction seemed to be just what Drakon needed to get his footing once more.

"Argh!" Drakon lunged at Kyril, tackling him down to the ground.

Kyril yelled again, the blade in his back going deeper then the handle broke off. Both men tumbled and ended up going down a sand hill. Panic set in, helping her to crawl to the side and watching the two of them kept rolling down.

"Drakon!" she yelled.

Both men reached the bottom but neither stood up. Instead, they struggled with each other and kept rolling. Light shined off from another blade in Kyril's hand.

"No!" she screamed.

Kyril somehow got the upper hand. He rolled to the top and was trying to press the knife into Drakon's throat. Drakon grabbed Kyril's wrists with both hands. She could see the power in both of them. The strain on their arms, muscles bulging, one trying to push down, the other holding him off.

She held her breath, didn't know what to do and bit her lip to stop herself from crying out. Amelia feared if she did, then she might distract Drakon and he didn't need that.

"Once my blade pierces your heart, my cock will find a new home in your whore," Kyril sneered.

With a growl, Drakon somehow managed to flip them over, and Kyril was now on the bottom. Amelia couldn't see the knife, had no clue if it was still between them pointing at Drakon's chest or not.

They both yelled and the straining that was between them suddenly stopped. Amelia lost her restraint and screamed, staring down at the two, holding her breath, waiting to see which one was going to stand up.

Drakon staggered to his feet and her gut dropped. She saw blood on his hands, his face white and just knew without a doubt that the knife must have gone into him after all. However when he took two steps backwards, she saw differently. Kyril lay on the ground, the knife that he tried to stick in Drakon now sticking out from the middle of his chest, blood pouring from it, turning the golden sand red.

"Drakon," she breathed out.

Drakon looked up at her, his breathing come fast. He turned and jogged up the hill right to her where he pulled her into his arms, holding her tight. Unable to control herself, Amelia broke down crying. She couldn't stop the tears or prevent them from falling.

"I've got you," he said softly.

It took her a few moments before she was able to pull away from him and look over her shoulder. "Ismame."

Taking her hand, Drakon stood up, helping her. They walked over to where Ismame lay. Her eyes were closed, blood on her belly, no life in her body at all.

"She tried to save me from him," she whispered.

"If she didn't take you to him then there wouldn't be anything to save you from."

Amelia looked up at him. "We can't leave her here."

Drakon nodded, "Go get Kyril's horse. We'll use that."

He did all the work. Drakon wrapped Ismame up in a blanket Kyril had on the back of his horse, slung Ismame's body over it, and then placed Amelia on his horse, swinging himself up behind her. With a nudge and slight kick, the horse took off at a run, leaving Kyril's dead body where it lay.

Drakon held her tight against his chest and she welcomed the embrace, even though it hurt like hell on her backside. The sun began to set by the time they reached the palace and Amelia was a bit shocked to see all the men that had gathered there.

Pulling the horse to a stop, he got off before it completely stopped and helped her down. Alexis came out.

"You found her!" He smiled, but that smile disappeared when he spotted the body on the other horse. "No," Alexis went over to it, pulled the blanket from the head. His shoulders slumped. "Ismame," he whispered.

"Are the men ready?" Drakon asked.

Alexis dropped his head, touching his forehead to the back of Ismame's. "I didn't want her death."

"Alexis, Kyril is dead," Drakon said. That seemed to snap Alexis out of his grief. "We need to get the others before they find out."

"What? No!" Amelia grabbed Drakon's shirt. "You can't go, please!" Tears once more came to her eyes and fell down her face.

"I have to take care of him," he told her, wrapping his arms around her, pressing her close.

Amelia pressed her face into his chest. "Don't leave me."

Drakon pulled back, cupped her chin, and had her looking up at him. "I have to do this, Amelia. If we don't get those men out of here, they'll attack. I have to do this."

"I'm afraid," she whispered.

"I know, and I promise you as soon as I return, I'll never leave your side again." He bent down kissing her lightly.

"Promise?"

"With all my heart." He pulled away from her, turned, and was back up on his horse.

Alexis came up to her, hand on shoulder. "Will you see to the burial?"

She nodded and he turned away. "I'll take care of it. Alexis." Alexis stopped his back still to her. "She died saving me. She never meant for Kyril to do this, she only wanted the throne."

He nodded and finished walking away from her. Amelia stood on the steps, watching Drakon, Alexis and the men head away from the palace towards the camp that Kyril had set up. She stayed there until she couldn't see them anymore.

Only one maid lived through the raid and she saw to Amelia's needs. She helped clean her, tend to any wounds, and then slip into her long white silk robe, since it was the lightest. of cloth After Amelia was done, she ate then went to seeing to the preparations of Ismame body.

Her sister rested on her bed, a thin sheet covering her white body. The servants that were left had already washed her and were now braiding her hair. They dressed her in the Roman style since that was how Amelia planned on burying her.

With darkness covering the land, a bright moon the only light in the sky, Amelia once more stood outside on the marble steps, staring out at the orange glow off in the distance. Fire burned in the campsite in the distance that Kyril had set up and she prayed that Drakon wasn't hurt.

How long she stood out there, she didn't know. Her maid came and took her to bed. Amelia was so tired that she didn't fight, didn't speak, only lay down on the soft bedding, and let her eyes close. She felt numb. How long she slept, she didn't know, either, but when she opened her eyes, Drakon was there.

Not a word was said. He stood in the doorway, dirty, bloody. Amelia slipped off the bed, walked up to him and meeting his eyes began to undress him, letting the clothing lay where they fell. Once she had him naked, she took his hands, walked backwards towards the large tub, pulling him with her. At the edge, she let go of his hands, unknotted her robe and let it drop as well, then took his hands once more and they moved into the cool water.

Drakon said nothing and she bathed him. She cleaned him of the blood, of the dirt, of death itself. Once he was clean, she again led him out, dried him off, and took him to her bed where he went willingly, laid down, and had her in his arms with a sigh.

"It's over?" she finally asked.

"It's over," he answered.

* * * *

Drakon followed behind the funeral march with the others as Amelia led her people down to the Valley of the Kings with Corydon's body. It had been almost a week since Corydon and Ismame were killed and in that time something changed within Amelia. She seemed to distance herself from everyone, including him. He told himself that it was grief, nothing more, and he prayed it was so.

Kyril's father showed up and Drakon was there to meet him, as were his men. The old man was escorted to the palace where Amelia waited for him. They talked alone, and when he came out it was to sign a treaty that clearly said if anyone from Drudent came to Egypt, again, death would also come swiftly. The old man left right after signing it with his son's body.

At the entrance to the tomb, Amelia preformed all the ancient rites for her brother. Servants took the sarcophagus deep into the mountain and the doorway was sealed. Later that night, Alexis put his wife to rest in the old custom by burning the body. Amelia stood still as stone, watching the body burn.

Drakon sat in the great hall, alone, sipping wine when Alexis joined him. He didn't feel like being around many people, just like Amelia.

"Is she alright?" Drakon asked.

"I don't know," Alexis, answered. "Her maid told me that she's sitting in front of the window, staring out at the river. She hasn't eaten a thing either or has slept much."

"She's the last of her people," Drakon sighed. "I know how she feels." He took a drink, rested his head back on the chair, eyes on Alexis. "She saw me kill him with my bare hands. I'm sure her feelings about me have changed."

"I think she's in love with you, just like you are with her."

"How do I take her pain away?" Drakon whispered.

"Go to her. Be there. It's all you can do. The Drudents took her family away, give her something back."

True to what Alexis told him, when Drakon entered Amelia's room she indeed sat on the floor in front of her window, staring out. A tray of food rested on her nightstand, untouched.

He entered quietly, locked the door, took his boots off and walked silently toward her. He stood behind her and looked out at the night as well.

"I wish I could say the words to make your pain go away," he said softly. "Wish like I hell I knew how to make it all stop, but I don't. What I can say is that I've been where you're at and it will get easier."

She surprised him by leaning back. Drakon wrapped his arms around her, chin on top of her head. "They've taken everything," she breathed out."

He heard the pain, the tremor in her voice and tightened his hold. "No, they've not taken everything."

"Don't leave me." A tear hit his arm and her voice shook.

"I'll never leave you."

"Promise."

Drakon turned her, saw the tears, and sat down on the bed, settling her on his lap, moving her legs around his hips. He reached up and wiped away her tears. "Marry me and I'll swear before your Gods that I'll never leave you. You're my heart, my soul, my everything. I fell in love with you when you were sixteen and I love you even more now. Marry me, Amelia, marry me."

She smiled. The first smile he'd seen since coming back after the fighting. Fresh tears fell and she kept on smiling. "I love you, Drakon."

"Is that a yes?"

She laughed, which sounded more like a giggle. "Yes. I'll marry you." He stood up, taking her with him, hugging her tight, and twirling her around. "Drakon stop, I have one small condition for you."

He stopped, but didn't put her down. "What?" One eyebrow went up with his question?

"Well it's more of two really."

"I'm listening."

"Okay, the first is that we marry tomorrow. I don't want to wait."

"I can do that, but it also depends on the second."

Her face turned red and her fingers threaded into his hair. "Well, I want one more night in your arms as, shall we say, a fallen woman."

It took Drakon a few second before what she said sunk it and when it did, he busted out laughing. He couldn't help it. "Oh, my dear, the gods surly favored me the day we met."

"Well, you know, we Egyptians have a small saying. Our fate is in the hands of the gods."

"And on that one I will never disagree with you. The fate of the gods shall always be a mystery to me." Amelia kissed him and Drakon moaned into the kiss, taking them both to the bed. He dropped down with her under him, breaking the kiss. "Now get ready my love, I'm going to love you so thoroughly tonight that we will never forget."

Amelia moaned, wiggled under him, and smiled. "I'm looking forward to it."